A MAN CALLED
HARRY BRENT

Francis Durbridge

WILLIAMS & WHITING

Titles by Francis Durbridge published by Williams & Whiting

1   The Scarf – tv serial
2   Paul Temple and the Curzon Case – radio serial
3   La Boutique – radio serial
4   The Broken Horseshoe – tv serial
5   Three Plays for Radio Volume 1
6   Send for Paul Temple – radio serial
7   A Time of Day – tv serial
8   Death Comes to The Hibiscus – stage play
    The Essential Heart – radio play
    (writing as Nicholas Vane)
9   Send for Paul Temple – stage play
10 The Teckman Biography – tv serial
11 Paul Temple and Steve – radio serial
12 Twenty Minutes From Rome – a teleplay
13 Portrait of Alison – tv serial
14 Paul Temple: Two Plays for Radio Volume 1
15 Three Plays for Radio Volume 2
16 The Other Man – tv serial
17 Paul Temple and the Spencer Affair – radio serial
18 Step In The Dark – film script
19 My Friend Charles – tv serial
20 A Case For Paul Temple – radio serial
21 Murder In The Media – more rediscovered serials and
    stories
22 The Desperate People – tv serial
23 Paul Temple: Two Plays for Television
24 And Anthony Sherwood Laughed – radio series
25 The World of Tim Frazer – tv serial
26 Paul Temple Intervenes – radio serial
27 Passport To Danger! – radio serial
28 The World of Tim Frazer – tv serial
29 Send For Paul Temple Again – radio serial

30) Mr Hartington Died Tomorrow

Murder At The Weekend – the rediscovered newspaper serials and short stories

Also published by Williams & Whiting:
Francis Durbridge : The Complete Guide
By Melvyn Barnes

Titles by Francis Durbridge to be published by Williams & Whiting

A Game of Murder
Breakaway – The Family Affair
Breakaway – The Local Affair
Farewell Leicester Square (writing as Lewis Middleton Harvey)
Five Minute Mysteries (includes Michael Starr Investigates and The Memoirs of Andre d'Arnell)
Johnny Washington Esquire
Melissa
Murder On The Continent (Further re-discovered serials and stories)
One Man To Another – a novel
Operation Diplomat
Paul Temple and the Alex Affair
Paul Temple and the Canterbury Case (film script)
Paul Temple and the Conrad Case
Paul Temple and the Geneva Mystery
Paul Temple and the Gilbert Case
Paul Temple and the Gregory Affair
Paul Temple and the Jonathan Mystery
Paul Temple and the Lawrence Affair
Paul Temple and the Madison Mystery
Paul Temple and the Margo Mystery
Paul Temple and the Sullivan Mystery
Paul Temple and the Vandyke Affair
Paul Temple: Two Plays For Radio Vol 2 (Send For Paul Temple and News of Paul Temple)
The Doll
The Female of the Species (The Girl from the Hibiscus and Introducing Gail Carlton)
The Man From Washington

The Passenger
Tim Frazer and the Salinger Affair
Tim Frazer and the Mellin Forrest Mystery

INTRODUCTION

Francis Durbridge (1912-98) was prominent among writers of mystery thrillers for BBC radio from the 1930s to the 1960s. As early as 1938 he found the niche in which he was to establish his name, when his radio serial *Send for Paul Temple* proved so successful that subsequent Paul Temple serials over several decades resulted in an enormous UK and European fanbase. It was therefore natural, while continuing to write for radio, that Durbridge should join the rush of writers into television – and he did so by writing the first thriller serial on UK television, *The Broken Horseshoe* (1952).

A Man Called Harry Brent is one of Durbridge's best and most intriguing television serials. It was his twelfth, shown in six thirty-minute episodes on BBC2 from 22 March to 26 April 1965, although it could legitimately be counted as his fourteenth because *The World of Tim Frazer* (1960-61) had consisted of three interlinked six-episode serials. Each episode of *A Man Called Harry Brent* was repeated on BBC2 later the same week and the serial was again repeated several years later, on BBC1 from 13 September to 18 October 1968.

The producer/director, Alan Bromly, had been since 1955 the guru for most of the Durbridge television serials, just as Martyn C. Webster had been for Durbridge's radio serials since the 1930s. The Durbridge/Bromly television partnership began impressively with *Portrait of Alison* in 1955, and they cemented their relationship by consistently teasing viewers with the many Durbridge elements that became so familiar – numerous red herrings, cliff-hanger endings to each episode, and the certainty that none of the characters should be believed whatever they might say.

In spite of the absence of Paul Temple, viewers were enthralled over a period of nearly thirty years by the gripping plots that made Durbridge the pre-eminent exponent of the thriller serial on UK television. There was no doubt that he was the master of the twist and turn, following the tortuous trail of a character caught in a web being unremittingly spun by a killer whose identity remained unknown until the dénouement. Then there was the added factor of "Britishness" that distinguished Durbridge from the numerous American television imports that relied upon "sock-in-the jaw" action, whereas with Durbridge there was often an air of normality until the bodies started piling up.

Although *A Man Called Harry Brent* was repeated on BBC1 in 1968, it took until 2016 for a DVD to be marketed - included in the box set *Francis Durbridge Presents Volume 1*, BBC/Madman, 2016. And the title of the set *Francis Durbridge Presents* is significant in itself, defining a crucial aspect of Durbridge's television career – because his success in television drama was monumental, with the result that for all his serials from 1960 (beginning with *The World of Tim Frazer*) the BBC gave him the unprecedented accolade of the "*Francis Durbridge Presents*" screen credit before the title sequence of each episode.

In spite of his Britishness, or probably because of it, Durbridge built an enviable reputation in Europe. His radio serials were broadcast in various countries from the late 1930s, in translation and using their own actors; and beginning with *The Other Man* (1959 in Germany as *Der Andere*) there was a swell of Continental television versions that attracted a huge body of viewers. So addictive was Durbridge on European radio and television that German commentators defined his serials as *straßenfeger* (street sweepers) because so many people stayed at home to listen to them on the radio or watch them on television.

In the case of *A Man Called Harry Brent*, the German television version was *Ein Mann namens Harry Brent* (15 – 19 January 1968, three episodes), translated by Marianne de Barde and directed by Peter Beauvais; the Italian television version was *Un certo Harry Brent* (1-17 November 1970, six episodes), translated by Franca Cancogni, adapted by Biagio Proietti and directed by Leonardo Cortese; the Polish television version was *Harry Brent* (1-15 June 1972, three episodes), translated by Kazimierz Piotrowski and directed by Andrzej Zakrzewski; and the French television version was *Un certain Richard Dorian* (23 November to 11 December 1973, sixteen episodes), translated and directed by Abder Isker. And according to IMDb there was also a Finnish television version entitled *Mies nimeltä Harry Brent*, but details have proved impossible to trace and this might have been simply the UK production dubbed into Finnish.

On UK television *A Man Called Harry Brent* had a superb cast – including, for his first and only role as a Durbridge protagonist, the Australian actor Edward Brayshaw (1933-90). But this raises the question – who was the leading man, Harry Brent or Detective Inspector Alan Milton? The role of Milton was in the safe hands of Gerald Harper (b.1929, though some sources say 1931), who achieved television stardom in *Adam Adamant Lives!* (1966-67) and *Hadleigh* (1969-76) but also took the lead in Durbridge's television serial *A Game of Murder* (1966) and in his West End plays *Suddenly at Home* (1971-73) and *House Guest* (1981-82). Nevertheless, among regular supporting actors in Durbridge television serials it is impossible to resist mentioning the wonderful Brian Wilde (1927-2008), who before his long comedy runs as Prison Officer Barrowclough in *Porridge* and Foggy Dewhurst in *Last of the Summer Wine* played serious and contrasting roles in Durbridge's *Portrait of Alison*, *The World of Tim Frazer* and *Melissa* before *A Man Called Harry Brent*.

As with many of Francis Durbridge's radio and television scripts, *A Man Called Harry Brent* was novelised (Hodder & Stoughton, November 1970). It appeared in Germany as *Ein Mann namens Harry Brent* and in Poland as *Harry Brent*. In the UK it has become a sought-after book, because copies of the Hodder first edition and the only reprint (Ian Henry, 1981) are scarce and expensive and it has not been produced as a paperback or audiobook.

Melvyn Barnes
Author of *Francis Durbridge: The Complete Guide* (Williams & Whiting, 2018)

This book reproduces Francis Durbridge's original script together with the list of characters and actors of the BBC programme on the dates mentioned, but the eventual broadcast might have edited Durbridge's script in respect of scenes, dialogue and character names.

A MAN CALLED HARRY BRENT

A Serial in Six Episodes

By FRANCIS DURBRIDGE

Broadcast on BBC2 Television 22 March – 26 April 1965

Produced and Directed by Alan Bromly

CAST:

Barbara Smith . . . . Audine Leith
Harry Brent . . . . Edward Brayshaw
Eric Vyner . . . . Bernard Brown
Gladys . . . . Penny Lambirth
Harold Tolly . . . . .Brian Wilde
Carol Vyner . . . . Jennifer Daniel
Thomas Fielding . . . . .Gerald Young
Det-Insp. Alan Milton . . . . Gerald Harper
Det-Sgt. Roy Philips . . . . Peter Ducrow
Tomlins . . . . .Christopher Wray
Bernard Wedgwood . . . . John Falconer
Olive . . . . .Winifred Dennis
Dr. Fess . . . . Michael Harding
Mrs. Tolly . . . . Marion Mathie
Mario . . . . Joseph Cuby
Jacqueline Dawson . . . . Judy Parfitt
Tony Moore . . . . James Locker
Kevin Jason . . . . .Alan Hockey
Reg Bryer . . . . John Horsley
Tom . . . . Denis Cleary
George . . . . Frank Barrie
Mrs. Green . . . . Anna Wing
Market stallholder . . . .Harry Davis
Market stallholder . . . . Hugh Halliday
Market stallholder . . . . .Stewart Guidotti

Mark Rainer . . . . Leon Shepperdson
Booth . . . . Brian Cant
Waiter . . . . .Ray Marioni
Waiter . . . . David J. Grahame
Brian Filey . . . . Michael Warren
Laidman .Richard Wilding
Stone . . . . Desmond Cullum-Jones
Policewoman . . . . Diana Chapman
Clayton . . . . .Fred Ferris
Sir Gordon Town . . . . Raymond Huntley
Waiter . . . . .Norman Atkyns
Policeman .Graham Ashley
Policeman .Stanley Walsh
Van driver . . . . Edward Webster
Waiter . . . . John Scott Martin

EPISODE ONE

THE FLOWERS

OPEN TO: The platform at a Main London Railway Station
An attractive GIRL has passed through the ticket barrier and is walking along the platform; her eyes searching the half empty carriages of a stationary train. The GIRL is wearing a dark brown suit with crocodile shoes and a matching handbag. She carries a bunch of flowers and a morning newspaper.

CUT TO: A First-Class compartment on the stationary train. There are two occupants of the carriage – an ELDERLY LADY and a pleasant looking MAN in the early thirties. They are strangers to each other.
The EDERLY LADY is reading a fashion magazine and the MAN – HARRY BRENT – is absorbed in a novel. The GIRL appears in the corridor and tries somewhat unsuccessfully, to open the door of the compartment. She is obviously handicapped by the flowers and the handbag she is carrying. HARRY BRENT glances up and, suddenly realising what is happening, leans forward and opens the door from the inside. As the GIRL enters the compartment she looks at HARRY and puts the flowers down on the empty seat opposite him.
GIRL: Thank you.
HARRY smiles at her.
GIRL: This – this does go to Market Weldon?
HARRY: I hope so.
The EDERLY LADY glances at HARRY, faintly amused by his reply, then looks across at the GIRL who is now settling into her seat. After a momentary hesitation HARRY BRENT closes the door and returns to his book.

CUT TO: Outside Market Weldon Railway Station.
Market Weldon is a small agricultural town about an hour and a half from London. There is a taxi rank and a car park

3

directly opposite the entrance to the station. The London train has arrived.

Passengers are pouring out of the station one of which is the GIRL with the flowers who approaches the taxi rank. She has a word with one of the drivers and gets into his cab. As the car draws away HARRY BRENT strolls out of the Station carrying a small weekend case. He looks up and down the road and then crosses towards the car park.

CUT TO: The Car Park at Market Weldon Station.

ERIC VYNER is sitting at the driving wheel of a Humber shooting break waiting for the arrival of HARRY BRENT. He suddenly sees HARRY coming across the car park and climbs out of the brake. ERIC – a shrewd and successful farmer in his early forties – has sprained his right wrist and is wearing a loose sling.

ERIC: Good morning, Harry!

HARRY: Hello, Eric! (*He notices the sling*) What's all this in aid of?   Carol didn't tell me you'd had an accident.

ERIC: It's nothing. I was acting the damn fool with a tractor – trying to show off in front of the men.

HARRY: (*Indicating the brake*) Can you drive all right?

ERIC: Yes, of course! Drive any damn thing! Jump in, old man!

HARRY smiles and gets into the brake as does ERIC and he drives off.

CUT TO: Inside ERIC VYNER's shooting brake.

HARRY BRENT and ERIC are sitting side by side.

HARRY: Are you sure it's all right, Eric – my staying the weekend, I mean?

ERIC: Good heavens, yes! I've told you Harry – when you and that sister of mine get married I shall expect you every weekend.

HARRY: (*Smiling*) If you're not careful we shall be moving in on you!

ERIC: And why not, for Pete's sake? We're only an hour and a half from Town. You could travel up every day as easy as pie. It'd stop all this flap-doodle about not being able to find a flat.

HARRY: I've found one; at least I think so. I want Carol to take a look at it one day next week, if she can manage it.

ERIC: No reason why she shouldn't; old man Fielding is awfully good about her having time off. In any case, she finishes with him next week.

HARRY: Yes, I know.

ERIC: My goodness, Thomas Fielding is going to miss Carol. She's been a damn good secretary to him.

HARRY: Yes, and I should imagine he's been a very good boss.

ERIC: Oh, very!

HARRY: How long has she been with the firm, Eric?

ERIC: Oh – must be getting on for seven years. She's been Fielding's secretary for nearly five years. (*He looks at his watch*) Have you time for a quick one, Harry?

HARRY: Yes, I think so.

ERIC: We'll pop in The Bear.

HARRY: Good idea. Then I can stroll round to Fielding's, it's just round the corner.

ERIC: Don't you trust my driving, old boy?

HARRY: (*Looking at the sling*) I'm not mad about it at the best of times.

ERIC laughs.

CUT TO: The Bar Parlour of The Bear Hotel, Market Weldon.

HAROLD TOLLY is standing at the bar chatting to GLADYS, the barmaid.

TOLLY: … Of course it was ridiculous – damn ridiculous – he'd been wearing the tie, it was obvious …

GLADYS: Well, what did you say to her?

TOLLY: I said: My dear Mrs Croft-Wallace, your husband may be on the council – he may be Chairman of the flipping Watch Committee for all I know – but I'm not changing that tie! You bought it – you paid for it – and you're stuck with it!

GLADYS: What happened?

TOLLY: She was stuck with it! Damn cheek. You know what it is, they think just because you've got a stall in the market they can take advantage of you.

GLADYS: I can't imagine anyone taking advantage of you, Mr Tolly.

TOLLY: You'd be surprised, Gladys. Still – I'm open to offers.

GLADYS: (*Significantly*) How's Mrs Tolly these days?

TOLLY: (*Laughing*) You would bring that up! She's around. She's around some place …

ERIC enters with HARRY. He indicates a corner table as he crosses to the bar.

ERIC: Scotch, Harry?

HARRY: Thank you, Eric.

HARRY crosses to the table.

ERIC: (*At the bar*) A large Scotch and a Gin and tonic, Gladys.

GLADYS: Thank you, Mr Vyner.

ERIC: Hello, Tolly! How's business?

TOLLY: Can't grumble, I suppose. My word, that's a nice tie you're wearing, Mr Vyner!

ERIC: Don't give me that malarkey, you know damn
           well I bought it from that stall of yours.
TOLLY: (*Laughing*) I was going to give you a ring this
           morning. I'm opening a new place over at Byfleet,
           and I'm looking for some timber; nothing fancy
           just …
ERIC: (*Cutting him short*) Try Greatrex at Esher, he'll
           probably fix you up.
TOLLY: Yes, I hadn't thought of that. That's a good idea –
           a very good idea. Thanks. Can I buy you a drink?
ERIC: Not at the moment, thank you, Tolly.

ERIC takes the drinks and returns to HARRY who is now
sitting at the table. HARRY is looking at TOLLY.

ERIC: (*Putting the drinks on the table*) Would you like
           some soda, or do you want it neat, as usual?
HARRY: This is fine.
ERIC: (*Sitting down*) There must be Scots blood in you,
           Harry.
HARRY: Indian, old boy. Navajo.
ERIC: Where are you having lunch?
HARRY: Haven't the faintest idea. This is on Fielding.
ERIC: Really? I didn't know that.
HARRY: Yes, he's invited us out – a sort of fond farewell to
           Carol.
ERIC: It's very nice of him.
HARRY: Yes, it is. How's he getting on, by the way? Has
           he got a new secretary lined up?
ERIC: No, I don't think so. I gather it's a bit of a
           problem. He's still interviewing people.
           Incidentally, what do you make of him – what do
           you think of the old boy?
HARRY: I don't really know him, Eric. I only met him for
           the first time last week. (*Amused*) I must say he
           took me by surprise.

7

ERIC: What do you mean?

HARRY: He looked me straight in the eye and said: "You're pinching the best secretary I've ever had, young man – but thank God she's not marrying that policeman!" (*Laughing*) I hadn't the slightest idea what he was talking about.

ERIC: Hadn't Carol told you about the ex-boyfriend?

HARRY: Yes, but I'd forgotten he was with the C.I.D.

ERIC: (*Shaking his head*) Fielding never liked Alan. (*Raising his glass*) Well – here's to you, Harry – and Carol …

HARRY: Thank you, Eric.

HARRY raises his glass.

CUT TO: The Private Office of Thomas Fielding.

This is a large, well equipped "lived in" office. THOMAS FIELDING has spent a great deal of his life in this office. Apart from the usual paraphernalia there are many of THOMAS's personal belongings (pipe racks, photographs, an old sports jacket on a hanger, a dilapidated golf bag, etc) Things which one would not normally find in the office of a successful executive. There are two doors: one leading to the general office and a second door, down right, to the board room.

THOMAS FIELDING is sitting at his desk reading a letter. A vigorous, healthy-looking man in his early sixties. His secretary – CAROL VYNER – enters from the outer office and places half a dozen letters on the desk.

CAROL: (*Indicating letters*) Here's the second post. There's nothing important. Oh – that girl doesn't want the job, after all. The one you interviewed yesterday.

THOMAS: The one with the big – chest?

CAROL: Yes.

8

THOMAS: I'm delighted to hear it. She couldn't spell and her manners were atrocious.

CAROL: You're seeing a Miss Barbara Smith at twelve-thirty and another girl this afternoon at a quarter past four.

THOMAS rises from the desk, glancing at his watch as he does so.

THOMAS: What time is Harry supposed to be here?

CAROL: I told him any time after twelve; the train's probably late.

THOMAS: They usually are these days. Incidentally, I went up to Town on Tuesday night. You'll never guess who I travelled with.

CAROL looks at him.

THOMAS: Your ex-boyfriend.

CAROL: Alan?

THOMAS: (*Nodding*) Detective Inspector Alan Milton.

CAROL: He seems to be going up to Town quite a lot lately. Harry and I bumped into him about a week ago.

THOMAS: (*Moving down to her*) You know, it's very funny, Carol. When you were friendly with Milton, I just couldn't stand him. I thought him a supercilious devil without an idea in his head. Now – I'm not so sure.

CAROL: Alan's an easy man to under-rate.

THOMAS: Yes, I think perhaps he is.

There is a knock – the office door opens – and HARRY BRENT pops his head into the room.

HARRY: May I come in?

CAROL: Hello, darling!

HARRY crosses and kisses CAROL on the cheek.

HARRY: (*To THOMAS*) Good morning, sir. I hope I'm not too early?

THOMAS:	(*Shaking hands*) No, of course not. How are you, Harry?
HARRY:	I'm fine. And you, sir?
THOMAS:	Oh – still having secretary trouble.
CAROL:	He doesn't mean me, darling.
HARRY:	I know what he means.

THOMAS *FIELDING crosses towards the board room door.*

THOMAS:	Let's have a drink in the board room – then we'll go out and have a bite to eat. I've booked a table at The Grand.
CAROL:	You've got Miss Smith at half past twelve.
THOMAS:	Oh, Lord – yes. I was forgetting that.

The internal phone rings on FIELDING's desk and CAROL answers it.

CAROL:	(*On phone*) Yes? … Just a moment. (*To THOMAS*) Miss Smith is here – she's just arrived.
THOMAS:	Oh, good! Send her in, I'll see her straight away.
CAROL:	(*On phone*) Ask Miss Smith to come in.

Carol replaces the receiver.

THOMAS:	(*To CAROL*) Give Harry a glass of sherry, I'll join you in about five minutes.

THOMAS opens the board room door.

CAROL:	This girl's got some very good references, Mr Fielding, and she sounded very nice when she telephoned, so don't … (*She hesitates*)
THOMAS:	Don't what?
CAROL:	(*Smiling*) Well – I mean … She's probably as nervous as a kitten so do try to be nice to her.
THOMAS:	What do you mean – try and be nice to her? I am nice – I'm nice to everybody! Aren't I, Harry?

HARRY: I think so; but then I'm prejudiced – you're just
            going to buy me lunch.

*THOMAS laughs. There is a knock on the door and a junior
clerk shows BARBARA SMITH in. We have seen MISS SMITH
before; it is the girl on the train. She carries her handbag –
the flowers have obviously been disposed of. BARBARA
stands for a second looking across at HARRY BRENT, who is
obviously surprised to see her. The clerk goes out.*

HARRY: (*Pleasantly*) Why, hello!

BARBARA gives a little smile of recognition.

HARRY: (*To CAROL*) We met on the train.

THOMAS: Miss Smith, I'm Thomas Fielding – this is my
            secretary, Miss Vyner. Her fiancé, Mr Brent.

*Again BARBARA doesn't speak but gives a little nod. CAROL
moves a chair into position, facing the desk.*

CAROL: Do sit down, Miss Smith.

BARBARA: Thank you.

*She sits in the chair. CAROL speaks to THOMAS, indicating a
folder on his desk.*

CAROL: You'll find all the particulars in the folder, Mr
            Fielding – including Miss Smith's letter.

THOMAS: Thank you.

*THOMAS returns to his chair behind the desk. CAROL gives
BARBARA a reassuring smile and goes into the board room,
followed by HARRY. THOMAS clears his throat, opens the
manilla folder, and consults a typewritten letter.*

THOMAS: I see you've been in machine tools before,
            Miss Smith.

BARBARA: Yes, I worked for MacDowell and Company.

THOMAS: They're an excellent firm. When were you
            with them?

BARBARA: About three years ago.

THOMAS: In London?

BARBARA: London and Coventry.

11

THOMAS: (*Pleasantly*) And what did you do, exactly?

BARBARA: I started as a shorthand-typist in the Coventry office but after three months they made me secretary to a man called George Booth. Mr Booth's the Personnel Manager …

THOMAS: I know George Booth! We used to play golf together. A dapper little man with a toothbrush moustache.

BARBARA: That's right.

THOMAS: Terrible golfer.

BARBARA: I'm afraid I wouldn't know about that.

THOMAS: No, of course not. (*Smiling*) Go on, Miss Smith – tell me a little more about yourself.

BARBARA: Well – after I left MacDowell's I went to work for a firm of stock-brokers – Hadley and Salter – they're in Fenchurch Street.

The phone rings on the desk.

BARBARA: I didn't like this very much because the job was very different from what I'd been used to …

BARBARA breaks off as THOMAS picks up the phone.

THOMAS: Excuse me. (*On phone*) Hello? … Who? … All right – put him on. (*To BARBARA*) I'm sorry about this; it won't take a minute. (*On phone*) Hello, Fred – how are you? … Yes, the estimate's in the post – you should get it first thing tomorrow morning … (*Laughing*) Well, I think it's a ruddy marvel, I don't know how we're going to do it at the price … All right, phone me when you've had a look at it … No, don't do that, phone me … (*Amused*) I hope so, too, Fred. Thanks for ringing …

12

He replaces the phone and turns towards BARBARA again. His smile freezes. She has taken a gun from her handbag; it is pointing at THOMAS. Her expression is deadly serious. A stunned THOMAS FIELDING slowly rises.

THOMAS: What – what is this? (*Frightened*) What the hell are you doing with that gun?

CUT TO: The Board Room.

An oak panelled room, adjoining THOMAS FIELDING's office. The room is used for meetings, private luncheons, the occasional cocktail party. There is a large oval shaped table, an antique cabinet, and several comfortable chairs.

CAROL and HARRY BRENT are standing by the cabinet drinking sherry.

HARRY: … The snag, of course, is the bathroom, but once we move in I thought I'd have a word with the landlord and see if we can't do something about it.

CAROL: But the whole thing sounds marvellous, darling! How on earth did you hear about it?

HARRY: You remember that flat on the Finchley Road? The one where the old lady …

As HARRY speaks there is the sound of a gun shot from the adjoining office. HARRY stares at CAROL in astonishment then drops his glass and rushes towards the door.

CUT TO: THOMAS FIELDING's Office.

The board room door is thrown open and HARRY rushes into the office with CAROL. They stop dead. THOMAS FIELDING is lying on the floor by the side of his desk. BARBARA SMITH stands, gun in hand, staring down at the body. She appears dazed and confused as she holds on to the back of her chair. She very slowly turns her head as HARRY BRENT moves down towards the dead man.

13

CUT TO: DETECTIVE INSPECTOR ALAN MILTON's office at C.I.D. (County) Headquarters.

ALAN MILTON is sitting at his desk talking to DETECTIVE SERGEANT ROY PHILIPS. ALAN is a serious, faintly aggressive looking man in his thirties. PHILIPS wears his outdoor clothes and is perched somewhat precariously on the arm of a chair. He is older than ALAN and would be well advised to diet. BARBARA SMITH's handbag is on the desk and also the manilla folder previously seen in FIELDING's office.

ALAN: … Are you sure about this?

PHILIPS: Positive.

ALAN: Who did you talk to at MacDowell's?

PHILIPS: I spoke to the Secretary of the Company, and a man called George Booth; he's the Personnel Manager.

ALAN: (*Indicating the folder*) She's supposed to have worked for Booth.

PHILIPS: (*Shaking his head*) He's never heard of her, sir. I gave them a detailed description of the girl and Booth rang me back about half an hour ago. Both he and the secretary are confident she never worked for MacDowell's.

ALAN: And the stockbroker's?

PHILIPS: Precisely the same story – they've never heard of   her either. (*Pointing to the folder*) I'm afraid the letter she wrote to Fielding – and the references – they're just a pack of lies, Inspector.

ALAN opens the folder and stares at the letter.

ALAN: What about the hotel? She wrote to Fielding on hotel notepaper?

PHILIPS: (*Nodding*) The Clifton Hotel, Southampton Row. She arrived last Tuesday and checked

14

	out this morning. (*Consults his notebook*) She gave her permanent address as thirty-four Genoa Mansions, Kensington.
ALAN:	Well?
PHILIPS:	Have you ever heard of Genoa Mansions, sir?
ALAN:	No, but that doesn't mean ...
PHILIPS:	Neither have I; neither has anyone else, I'm afraid!

ALAN rises and moves down in front of his desk.

ALAN:	(*Angrily*) What the hell was this girl up to, Philips?

The telephone rings.

ALAN:	She checked into a London hotel, gave a false address – ten to one a false name – then applied for a job outside ... (*He snatches up the phone*) ... Hello? ... Speaking ... (*Irritated*) Who is that? (*With a glance to PHILIPS*) Oh, I'm sorry, sir, I didn't recognise your voice! ... Yes, we are, sir ... We are indeed ... But she refuses to talk, sir – she just won't say anything – not a word ... (*Annoyed*) Superintendent, I was with her for forty minutes and Dr Clayton spent the best part of an hour trying to persuade ... (*Barely controlling himself*) But-we-don't-know-who-she-is, that's just the point, sir! ... Yes, of course ... Of course ... We will indeed, sir ... Thank you, sir.

He replaces the receiver as TOMLINS, a uniformed police officer, enters from the outer office.

ALAN:	How in God's name that man ever became ... (*Seeing TOMLINS*) Yes – what is it?
TOMLINS:	The car's ready, sir.
ALAN:	Right. I'm just coming!

PHILIPS rises from the armchair. TOMLINS produces a notebook and pencil.

TOMLINS: Can I make the list now, sir?

ALAN: Yes, go ahead. (*To PHILIPS*) Check it with him, Sergeant. (*To TOMLINS*) Type six copies, the Superintendent wants four.

TOMLINS: Very good, sir.

ALAN takes his hat and coat out of a corner cabinet, mumbling to himself – "God knows why" – as he does so. He crosses to the door. PHILIPS moves down to the desk.

ALAN: I'll be back in an hour.

PHILIPS nods and ALAN goes. PHILIPS then picks up the handbag, opens it, and empties the contents onto the desk. We see: a powder compact; a theatre ticket; a crocodile purse; lipstick; a keyring with a Yale key and car key attached; an unopened packet of Gauloises cigarettes; and a lace handkerchief.

TOMLINS: What sort of fags are those?

PHILIPS: French. Ready?

TOMLINS: Okay.

PHILIPS: One packet of cigarettes. Gauloises. G-A-U-L-O-I-S-E-S …

TOMLINS: Thank you, Sergeant. I'm a lousy speller.

He writes in his notebook. PHILIPS looks at the theatre ticket.

PHILIPS: Theatre ticket. Dalesbury Repertory Theatre – Saturday, November fourteenth; Row D, seat number four. (*Thoughtfully*) November fourteenth, that's next weekend, isn't it?

TOMLINS: (*Looking up*) Today's the sixth. Yes, that's right.

PHILIPS hesitates, his thoughts on the ticket, then puts it down and picks up the purse.

PHILIPS: Crocodile purse … (*Opens purse*) Contents … Three fivers and a ten-shilling note … No,

16

wait a minute! (*Looks in the purse*) ... Yes, that's right. Three fivers and a ten-bob note.

TOMLINS continues writing in his book.

CUT TO: The living room of "Becklehurst Farm". This is the main room in a large farmhouse on the outskirts of Market Weldon. There are two doors in the room – the first leading to the hall, the second to ERIC VYNER's study.

CAROL is lying on the settee, still obviously distressed by the turn of events. HARRY sits next to her, at the foot of the settee, facing ERIC VYNER who is slumped in an armchair sucking his pipe. ALAN MILTON stands facing the three of them, his back to the huge fireplace.

ALAN: Carol, I know exactly how you must feel – but do try to be helpful, my dear.

He moves down to the settee.

ALAN: Now I want you to tell me what happened. Start at the beginning.

HARRY is faintly irritated by ALAN's manner.

HARRY: But she doesn't know what happened. She was with me – in the board room – when the shots were fired.

ALAN: Yes, I appreciate that, but I'd still like to hear what Carol's got to say.

CAROL is hesitant and still near to tears.

CAROL: When I told Mr Fielding that I was leaving to get married he put an advertisement in The Times. One Wednesday morning we had a letter from this girl – Barbara Smith. She phoned me in the afternoon to see if we'd received the letter and I made an appointment for her to see Mr Fielding.

ALAN: Where did she phone from?

17

CAROL:	From London, I think. I'm not sure where exactly.
ALAN:	(*Nodding*) When you told Mr Fielding about the appointment did he give you the impression that he knew Miss Smith, that he'd met her before in fact?
CAROL:	No, of course he didn't! (*She shakes her head*) He hadn't met her before, Alan, I'm sure of it! (*To HARRY*) You saw the girl, Harry – you saw her come into the office. Did you get the impression that they'd met before?
HARRY:	No, I certainly didn't.
CAROL:	(*Distressed*) He'd never set eyes on the wretched girl until this morning, I'm absolutely convinced of that, Alan!
ALAN:	(*Gently*) Yes, all right, Carol.
HARRY:	As a matter of fact, I was the one who'd seen her before.

ALAN turns and looks at HARRY, obviously surprised.

ERIC:	You, old boy?
HARRY:	(*To ALAN*) She was on the train, in the same compartment – she sat opposite me.
ALAN:	Did you speak to her?
HARRY:	She spoke to me. She had some flowers in her hand and she couldn't get the door open. I opened it for her, and she thanked me.
ALAN:	And that was all?
HARRY:	Yes. Oh – she asked me if the train was going to Market Weldon and I said it was.
ALAN:	Had you seen this girl before – before she got on the train, I mean?
HARRY:	No, never.
ALAN:	You're sure?

HARRY: Yes, I'm quite sure.

ALAN gives a little nod and returns to the fireplace.

ALAN: Well, that doesn't help us a great deal, I'm afraid. (*To CAROL*) We've talked with your friends at the office, we've seen Mrs Green, Thomas Fielding's housekeeper, we've even contacted his Club. No-one's ever heard of this girl.

ERIC: And what about Miss Smith herself?

ALAN: She just refuses to talk, Eric; won't say a word. It's no use, we simply can't get anything out of her.

HARRY: Does she seem upset at all?

ALAN: That's a difficult question to answer because she just doesn't say anything. I wouldn't say she was upset exactly; disturbed perhaps.

ERIC: Is her name Barbara Smith?

ALAN: (*Shrug*) You tell me.

HARRY: The thing that puzzles me is the time element. The train arrived at a quarter past eleven and she picked up a taxi straight away. Yet she didn't arrive at Fielding's until half past twelve. Eric met me off the same train, we had a drink, and yet I was at Fielding's before she was.

ALAN: That's perfectly true. But the taxi didn't take her to Fielding's, it took her to Halford Bridge.

ERIC: (*Surprised*) Halford Bridge? That's on the other side of town.

ALAN: Yes. When they reached the bridge, she dismissed the car and disappeared.

ERIC: And what time was this?

ALAN: About a quarter to twelve. Twenty-five minutes later she was seen in the High Street; she picked up another cab and drove out to Fielding's.

19

HARRY: So the big question is – what was she doing between a quarter to twelve and ten past?

ALAN: (*Shaking his head*) We know what she was doing; she was visiting someone.

ERIC: (*Puzzled*) But how do you know that?

ALAN: (*To ERIC*) She had the flowers when she left the train and she had them when she took the first taxi. But she hadn't got them when she arrived at Fielding's.

HARRY: Because she'd given them to someone?

ALAN: Right, Mr Brent. (*To ERIC*) So the big question is – who? Who did she give them to?

CAROL: (*After a moment; thoughtfully*) Alan, is there a hospital or a nursing home near Halford Bridge?

ALAN: No, I'm afraid there isn't, Carol. (*Smiling*) We did think of that.

ERIC: (*Sucking his pipe*) There's a cemetery, of course.

ALAN turns towards ERIC again, obviously surprised by the remark.

ALAN: A cemetery?

ERIC looks up; almost apologetically.

ERIC: Yes … I was just thinking. You know, flowers – cemetery … It's about five minutes' walk from Halford Bridge.

CUT TO: The Entrance to a small cemetery near Market Weldon.

A police car arrives and draws to a standstill near a tiny lodge at the entrance to the cemetery. The lodge is occupied by BERNARD WEDGWOOD, the cemetery superintendent, and his wife. ALAN gets out of the police car and is crossing towards the cemetery when WEDGWOOD comes out of the lodge carrying a wreath.

ALAN: Good evening, Mr Wedgwood!

WEDGWOOD: Yes?

ALAM: I'm Detective Inspector Milton, sir. Could you spare me a moment?

WEDGWOOD: Certainly.

ALAN: I'm making inquiries about a girl called Barbara Smith. I think perhaps she visited the cemetery this morning between eleven-forty and twelve-fifteen.

WEDGWOOD: Well, if she did, I probably saw her. I was on duty until three o'clock.

ALAN: A rather good-looking girl; about twenty-five or six; dark, fairly tall. She was wearing a brown suit with crocodile shoes and a handbag to match.

WEDGWOOD: I remember the girl! That's right – about five minutes to twelve. She had some flowers, and she was looking for a grave.

ALAN: Did she find it?

WEDGWOOD: Yes – I showed it to her.

ALAN: Would you be kind enough to show me the grave, Mr Wedgwood?

WEDGWOOD: Yes, certainly.

WEDGWOOD puts the wreath down, leaving it against the door of the lodge, then walks along a path into the cemetery. ALAN follows him.

CUT TO: The Cemetery.

BERNARD WEDGWOOD and ALAN come down a path. They reach a grave and WEDGWOOD stops and points towards the headstone, indicating that this is the grave ALAN wanted to see. We see the flowers carefully arranged in a stone vase, and the inscription on the headstone. It is the inscription that interests ALAN. It says, "In Beloved Memory of DAVID and FREDA BRENT, March 19th 1964".

CUT TO: The living room of Becklehurst Farm.

ALAN MILTON is shown into the room by OLIVE, ERIC VYNER's housekeeper. OLIVE is a buxom little woman in her early sixties.

OLIVE: I don't think they'll be long, Mr Milton; I was expecting them back before now.

ALAN: Where have they gone, Olive – do you know?

OLIVE: I think they've popped over to Mr Fielding's place, sir. Miss Carol wanted to see how Mrs Green was getting on.

ALAN: How is Carol?

OLIVE: She's a little better now, but she had a very bad night I'm afraid.

ALAN: Yes, I expect she did.

OLIVE: What a dreadful thing to have happened, sir. He was such a nice man, Mr Fielding.

ALAN: Yes, Olive. Is Mr Brent still here?

OLIVE: Yes, indeed, sir. They all went out together. Is there anything I can get you, Mr Milton? Would you like a nice cup of tea?

ALAN: No, thank you, Olive.

As ALAN speaks there is the sound of a car driving into the courtyard and he turns and crosses towards the window.

CUT TO: Becklehurst Farm.

ERIC's shooting brake has come to a standstill in the picturesque courtyard. In the foreground we see a wrought iron gate set in a brick wall and a well-kept path leading up to the front door of a large, rambling but by no means dilapidated farmhouse. About fifty yards or so to the left of the house stand the various out-buildings, including a double-fronted garage. An Austin Mini is parked in the courtyard near the wrought iron gate. HARRY BRENT has been driving the Humber and he remains at the wheel as ERIC and CAROL climb out of the car. CAROL notices the Mini.

CAROL: That's Alan's car.

ERIC: Yes, so it is.

ERIC turns to HARRY and indicates the brake.

ERIC: Don't bother to put it away, Harry – I'll see to it later.

HARRY: No, that's all right, Eric. I'll do it.

CAROL: I'll come with you, darling.

HARRY: There's no need, Carol. It won't take a minute.

HARRY glances across at the Mini as he changes gear and the Humber moves forward.

CUT TO: The living room of Becklehurst Farm.

ALAN is standing by the window, looking out into the courtyard. He turns as ERIC and CAROL enter the room.

ERIC: Hello, Alan! Nice to see you.

ALAN: Good afternoon, Eric. Carol …

CAROL: We've been over to Mr Fielding's, to see his housekeeper.

ALAN: Yes, I know. Olive told me. I saw Mrs Green yesterday, just for a few minutes.

CAROL: She's not my favourite woman but I must admit she's stood up to this pretty well. Better than I have, I'm afraid.

ALAN helps her off with her coat.

ALAN: Perhaps she wasn't as fond of Fielding as you were.

ERIC: Didn't Olive offer you a drink?

ALAN puts the coat on a chair.

ALAN: Yes – yes, thank you.

CAROL: (*To ERIC, with a faint smile*) You know Alan – when he's on duty.

ERIC: Are you on duty, old boy?

23

ALAN: Well – in a way, yes; I suppose I am. I'd like to have a word with your fiancé, Carol.

ERIC: He's putting the car away, he'll be here in a minute.

CAROL: What is it you want to see Harry about?

ALAN: Carol, we know absolutely nothing about this girl – Barbara Smith – so naturally I've got to make as many inquiries as possible.

ERIC: She still refuses to talk?

ALAN: I'm afraid so, Eric. She just won't say anything.

CAROL: Yes, but why do you want to see Harry? (*Shaking her head*) He doesn't know this girl; he told you yesterday.

ALAN: Yes, I know he did, but – (*Hesitant*) Carol forgive my asking but – where did you first meet Harry Brent?

CAROL: (*Surprised by the question*) Where did I meet him?

ALAN: Yes. (*Quickly; smiling*) Now I know what you're going to say! What on earth has this got to do with …

CAROL: That's precisely what I was going to say!

ALAN: You don't have to answer the question if you don't want to, Carol. But I'd be grateful if you would.

CAROL hesitates a moment.

CAROL: Last summer, after you and I – after we broke things off – I felt pretty miserable.

ALAN: (*Quietly*) You weren't the only one, Carol …

CAROL: (*Ignoring his remark*) Mr Fielding told me to go away for a couple of weeks. One Saturday morning I went into a travel bureau in Kensington. Harry was behind the counter …

ERIC: She thought he was one of the assistants, old boy – it turned out he owned the business.

ALAN: (*To CAROL; ignoring ERIC*) Go on …
CAROL: When I gave him my address, he told me that he
          came from this part of the world and we got
          talking about Market Weldon. A week later he
          rang me up – we had dinner together.
ALAN: I see. (*A pause*) It was as simple as that?
CAROL: (*Quietly*) Yes – as simple as that, Alan.

*ERIC stands, a shade embarrassed, not sure whether to look
at CAROL or ALAN.*

CUT TO: Brecklehurst Farm.

*HARRY BRENT has now parked the Humber in the garage
and, after closing the sliding doors, he turns and starts
walking back towards the house. He has gone about twenty
yards back and has reached the brick wall when he stops and
takes out a packet of cigarettes. He puts a cigarette in his
mouth and feels in his pocket for his lighter. Suddenly,
instinctively, he becomes aware of the fact that there is
someone behind him and he half turns but he is too late. A
gloved hand holding a large brick strikes HARRY on the back
of the head and he collapses.*

CUT TO: The living room of Becklehurst Farm.

*HARRY is on the settee, slowly recovering from his
experience in the courtyard. CAROL is sitting by his side,
anxiously propping him up with cushions as ALAN gives him
sips of brandy. ERIC stands watching, thoughtfully sucking
his pipe.*

ALAN: (*To CAROL*) He's all right now – he's coming
          round.
HARRY: My God, my head! (*He looks at CAROL, then up
          at ERIC*) What happened?
ERIC: We wondered what on earth had happened to you,
          Harry. We found you in the yard.

HARRY: I'd just put the car away and was walking towards the house when (*Wincing*) Gosh, he must have hit me with a brick or something.

ERIC: It was a brick, old boy!

CAROL: (*To ERIC*) I think we'd better let the doctor take a look at him, Eric.

HARRY: No, no, I'll be all right in a minute, Carol!

ALAN: Did you see who it was that hit you?

HARRY: No, I didn't see anything. I suddenly heard a noise behind me and then … (*He feels in his inside pocket*) My wallet's gone!

ERIC: Are you sure?

HARRY: (*Feeling in his pockets*) Yes. It's gone all right … (*Angrily*) It's the one you gave me, Carol. Damn – blast! …

ALAN: What was the wallet like, we'll get a description out straight away?

CAROL: (*To ALAN*) It's black with gold on the corners; it's got his initials on it.

HARRY: (*To ERIC*) There was fifty-five pounds in it …

ERIC: Oh, Lord …

ALAN: Anything else?

ERIC: Isn't that enough, old boy?

HARRY: … My driving license, some photographs; oh yes, and a letter from a travel bureau in Lucerne, but that's not important. It's the fifty-five quid I'm annoyed about.

HARRY sits up and removes one of the cushions.

CAROL: Are you feeling better?

HARRY: Yes, don't worry, Carol. (*Feeling his head*) I've got a headache, that's all.

ALAN gives HARRY the glass of brandy.

ALAN: Do you think you could answer one or two more questions, Mr Brent?

HARRY: I could try, but quite honestly, I just didn't see anything. One moment I was standing with a cigarette in my hand ...

ALAN: No, I don't mean about this afternoon, sir. (*He looks at HARRY*) You told me yesterday that you didn't know Barbara Smith – the girl that shot Thomas Fielding; that you'd never seen her until she got on the train.

HARRY: Yes; that's true. (*Puzzled*) Don't you believe me?

ALAN: (*Ignoring the question*) Mr Brent, I understand you were born in Market Weldon?

HARRY: Yes, in Richmond Street. (*Suddenly; irritated*) And for God's sake stop calling me <u>Mr</u> Brent.

ALAN: (*Ignoring the outburst*) Your father and mother – David and Freda Brent – were killed in a car accident. They're buried here, in the local cemetery.

HARRY: (*Puzzled*) Yes – well ... what about it?

ALAN: (*After a moment*) Eric was right – Barbara Smith did go to the cemetery yesterday morning. She went to the cemetery and she put the flowers she was carrying on your parents' grave.

HARRY slowly rises from the settee.

HARRY: She put the flowers on ... (*Shaking his head*) I don't believe this!

ALAN: It's true, sir.

HARRY: But – but why should she do that?

ALAN: I don't know why, Mr Brent.

CAROL and ERIC are looking at HARRY, both obviously surprised and puzzled by this information.

CUT TO: ALAN MILTON's Office.

TOMLINS is performing his usual Monday morning duties – rearranging the papers on ALAN's desk, changing the date on

27

the calendar (It is now Monday, 9th November), and sorting out the contents of the various trays. ALAN enters carrying a sheaf of papers; he appears to be irritable and faintly "on edge".

ALAN: Where the devil is Sergeant Philips, I've been looking all over for him?

TOMLINS: He's out, sir. We had a phone call from Harrison's, the scrap metal people – he went out almost immediately.

ALAN: What was the call about?

TOMLINS: I don't know, sir.

ALAN nods and moves to his chair at the desk.

TOMLINS: Is there anything I can do, sir?

ALAN: (*Dismissing him*) No, that's all right, Tomlins.

TOMLINS crosses to the door and as he goes out PHILIPS enters.

ALAN: Hello, Philips! What's all this about Harrison's?

PHILIPS produces HARRY BRENT's wallet from his inside pocket.

PHILIPS: Bill Harrison found this just over an hour ago. It was dumped in one of their bins.

ALAN: Is it Brent's?

PHILIPS: It's Brent's all right; apart from the initials, there's the letter he mentioned, and the driving license …

ALAN: But no money?

PHILIPS: No, I'm afraid not. The money's gone.

ALAN looks at him, arrested by his tone of voice.

ALAN: Is there anything else in the wallet?

PHILIPS: Yes, sir – there's this.

He takes a ticket out of the wallet.

ALAN: What is it?

PHILIPS: It's a theatre ticket … (*Studying ticket*) Dalesbury Repertory Theatre … Saturday, November the fourteenth … Row D, seat number (*He looks across at ALAN*) … five.

ALAN: (*Surprised*) But didn't that girl have –?

PHILIPS: This is the next seat, sir – the next seat at the same performance.

ALAN rises and moves down to PHILIPS.

ALAN: (*Quietly*) Let me have a look at that ticket …

ALAN takes the theatre ticket and examines it. After a little while he looks at PHILIPS, obviously curious, and puzzled by the ticket. He is about to say something when the phone rings. PHILIPS answers it.

PHILIPS: (*On phone*) Hello? … Yes … Yes, he's here …

He offers ALAN the phone.

ALAN: Who is it?

PHILIPS: It's Sergeant Craddock; he's steamed up about something …

ALAN: (*Taking the phone; on phone*) Hello, Craddock – what is it? … (*Stunned*) … Good God, when did this happen? … (*Angrily*) But how in hell's name did she get hold of the tablets in the first place? … Wasn't she searched? … Where are you taking her? … (*To PHILIPS, urgently*) Barbara Smith's taken poison, they're rushing her to a hospital. Get a car!

PHILIPS nods, puts down the wallet, and rushes out.

ALAN: (*On phone*) Which hospital? … Craddock, for God's sake – <u>which</u> hospital? … Tell the doctor I'm on the way!

(*ALAN slams down the receiver*)

CUT TO: A country road near Market Weldon.

An ambulance is racing down the road towards the main gates of the County Hospital. A police car suddenly appears – being driven at tremendous speed – and overtakes the ambulance.

CUT TO: The Main Entrance to the County Hospital.

The police car passes through the gates, followed by the ambulance, and races up the drive towards the hospital.

CUT TO: Outside the Hospital.

The police car has come to a standstill in front of the entrance to the casualty ward. ALAN and SERGEANT PHILIPS are standing by the Wolseley watching the approaching ambulance. As the ambulance draws to a standstill ALAN walks across to it, followed by PHILIPS. The rear doors of the ambulance are thrown open and Dr Fess – a neatly dressed little man – climbs down, followed by a uniformed nurse. The DOCTOR recognises ALAN and crosses to him.

DR FESS: Inspector Milton?

ALAN: Yes …

DR FESS: Dr Fess. I'm afraid we've got some bad news for you, Inspector. The patient's dead.

ALAN: (*Quietly; surprised*) Dead …?

DR FESS: I'm sorry, Inspector. We did everything we could, I assure you.

ALAN: Yes – yes, of course.

DR FESS: She was conscious for a little while and kept asking for someone.

ALAN looks at him.

DR FESS: A man called Harry Brent …

ALAN stares at the DOCTOR.

END OF EPISODE ONE

EPISODE TWO

JACQUELINE

OPEN TO: Becklehurst Farm.

A Mini-minor enters the yard and stops. ERIC VYNER comes out of the farmhouse and walks to the farmyard. He is carrying a briefcase and no longer wearing the sling. ALAN MILTON gets out of the Mini-minor.

ERIC: Hello, Alan!

ALAN: Good morning, Eric. You look very business-like!

ERIC: I've got a session with my accountant – supposed to be there at eleven.

ALAN: (*Laughing*) You'll have to be snappy, it's ten past now.

ERIC: Yes, I know! I'm always late these days.

ALAN: Is Harry Brent about, or has he gone back to London?

ERIC: No, Harry's still here, I don't think he's going back until this evening. (*He nods towards the house*) He's with Carol.

ALAN: How is Carol?

ERIC: She's not too good, old boy. Can't sleep. As a matter of fact the doc's been taking a look at her, he's only just left. (*Shaking his head*) There's been hell to pay, just because he won't let her go to the office.

ALAN: I can imagine it.

ERIC: Why do you want to see Harry?

ALAN: We've found his wallet.

ERIC: (*Obviously surprised*) Really, old boy? That's quick work … Well, I'm damned! Didn't think you people ever found anything.

ALAN: (*Smiling*) May I go in?

ERIC: Yes, of course, Alan! The door's open. See you later.

ALAN turns and walks towards the house.

CUT TO: The living room of Becklehurst Farm.

HARRY BRENT is sitting on the settee calmly watching his fiancée as, tense and 'on edge' she paces up and down the room. CAROL VYNER wears a dressing gown and slippers and as she turns and stubs out a cigarette in one of the ashtrays she finally gives vent to her feelings.

CAROL: … He's a silly old fool and if he had a grain of common-sense in that head of his he'd realise that …

HARRY: (*Interrupting*) He's an extremely good doctor and he knows precisely what he's doing.

He rises and crosses to her.

HARRY: Now relax, Carol, because no matter what you say you're not going to that office – not today at any rate.

CAROL: Harry, for heaven's sake don't be stupid! I've got to go to the office, if it's only for a couple of hours.

HARRY takes hold of CAROL's arm.

HARRY: Not today, Carol!

The door opens and ALAN enters.

ALAN: May I come in?

CAROL: (*Turning; surprised*) Why, hello, Alan!

She crosses down to him.

CAROL: Look, Alan – isn't it ridiculous, that wretched little doctor won't let me go to the office!

HARRY: (*To ALAN*) He's told her to take it easy, for today at any rate.

CAROL: (*Turning on HARRY*) But don't you understand they'll be in a terrible state at Fielding's! They just won't know which way to turn …

ALAN: I should do what the doctor says, Carol.

CAROL: You wouldn't do anything of the sort and you
           know very well you wouldn't. (*To HARRY*) I'll
           rest for a couple of hours and go down after
           lunch – you can run me there in the brake.
HARRY: (*Smiling*) We'll see about that.

ALAN takes the wallet out of his pocket.

ALAN: (*To HARRY*) We've found your wallet, but I'm
           afraid the money's missing. I'd like you to check
           the other things.

HARRY takes the wallet.

CAROL: Where did you find it?
ALAN: Someone dumped it in a bin at the back of
           Harrison's, the scrap metal people.
HARRY: (*Opening wallet*) Well, I didn't think I'd see this
           again.
ALAN: I'm sorry about the money.
HARRY: Yes, so am I …

HARRY examines the contents of the wallet.

ALAN: Is everything else there?
HARRY: Yes, it seems to be. There was nothing else of
           value, of course, apart from … Hello, what's
           this?

HARRY is looking at the theatre ticket.

ALAN: (*Watching HARRY*) It's a theatre ticket …
HARRY: Yes, I can see that. (*Shaking his head*) It's not
           mine. It doesn't belong to me.
ALAN: You mean – it wasn't in the wallet when it was
           stolen?
HARRY: No, it wasn't.
CAROL: But why should anyone put a theatre ticket in
           your wallet? It must be yours, Harry.
HARRY: (*Suddenly; almost angry*) I tell you it isn't! Do
           you think I don't know whether I was going to
           the theatre or not? (*Looks at ticket*) Dalesbury

Repertory Theatre … Why should I go out to Dalesbury, for heaven's sake? If I wanted to see a show, I'd go to one in the West End.

ALAN takes the ticket from him and looks at it.

ALAN: You're quite sure it's not yours?

HARRY: Yes, I'm absolutely sure. (*He looks at ALAN, curious*) Is there something odd about that ticket, apart from the fact that it was in my wallet?

ALAN: (*After a moment*) Barbara Smith had a theatre ticket in her handbag; the same theatre – same performance – the very next seat.

CAROL looks across at HARRY; puzzled.

HARRY: The next seat? You mean …

ALAN: D Four, Saturday, November fourteenth. This is Row D. Seat number Five.

HARRY: I – I don't believe this!

ALAN: It's true, Mr Brent.

CAROL looks at HARRY.

HARRY: Then, obviously, there's only one explanation. The person who stole the wallet put the ticket in it.

ALAN: You think that's what happened?

HARRY: Why, yes. (*Shaking his head*) I've certainly never seen that ticket before.

ALAN continues to stare at him for a moment, then he nods, apparently dismissing the matter.

ALAN: Right. Thank you.

CAROL: (*To ALAN*) Have you questioned the girl – Barbara Smith – about the ticket? It's possible that she might know how …

ALAN: (*Interrupting her*) I'm afraid we can't question Miss Smith about anything – she's dead.

CAROL: (*Stunned*) Dead?

ALAN: Yes, Carol …

38

HARRY: (*Quietly*) When did this happen?

ALAN: She committed suicide early this morning.

ALAN looks at HARRY for a moment, then at the theatre ticket he is still holding.

CUT TO: ALAN MILTON's flat in Market Weldon.

This is a bachelor flat over one of the shops in the High Street. A small flat consisting of an entrance hall, combined living-dining room, kitchen and bathroom. The flat is clean but distinctly untidy, there is a profusion of books and magazines.

ALAN lets himself into the flat and after hanging up his hat and coat in the hall crosses into the living room. He puts down the evening paper he is carrying, takes off his jacket, loosens his collar and tie, and then goes into the kitchen. He starts to pour himself a glass of milk when the phone starts to ring. He puts down the jug and, returning to the living room, answers the phone.

ALAN: (*On phone*) Market Weldon nine one three …

CUT TO: The telephone box outside the post office, Market Weldon.

MRS TOLLY is on the phone, struggling with her handbag and a collection of coins. She finally discovers the coin she requires and inserts it in the box. MRS TOLLY is a rather common, but by no means unattractive woman in her early thirties. She has a slight cockney accent. For the following conversation we switch back and forth between the phone box and ALAN MILTON's flat.

MRS TOLLY: (*On phone*) Is that nine one three?

ALAN: Yes …

MRS TOLLY: (*Obviously nervous*) Can – can I speak to Inspector Milton, please?

ALAN: This is Alan Milton speaking …

MRS TOLLY: Oh – my name's Tolly. Mrs Tolly. I used to work at Fielding's. We met last Christmas, Mr Milton, when your fiancée – Oh, I beg your pardon – when Miss Vyner …

ALAN: Yes, I remember you, Mrs Tolly. What can I do for you?

MRS TOLLY: Well – I've been reading about Mr Fielding; about the murder, I mean … (*Anxiously*) Do you think I could have a word with you sometime, Inspector? I'd rather not go down to the Station, if you don't mind.

ALAN: (*Pleasantly*) I'll be glad to see you, Mrs Tolly. Why don't you come here? I'm in the High Street – just above Jackson's the estate agents. You'll see the door, it's on the right-hand side.

MRS TOLLY: I know where it is. Can I come round straight away then?

ALAN: Yes, I shall be here all evening. Come whenever you feel like it.

MRS TOLLY: (*Relieved*) Oh, thanks … Thank you, Mr Milton.

MRS TOLLY replaces the receiver.

CUT TO: ALAN MILTON's flat. As before.

ALAN slowly replaces the receiver. He looks puzzled; curious – as he turns towards the kitchen again the front doorbell rings. He hesitates, then picks up his jacket and goes out into the hall and opens the front door. CAROL is in the doorway. She wears outdoor clothes and is carrying a large envelope.

ALAN: Good evening, Carol!

CAROL: I've just been to the office and I thought …

ALAN: No? You do surprise me! (*Laughing*) I knew
           you'd get your own way, Carol! You usually do.
CAROL: Alan, I didn't come here to be insulted!
ALAN: What did you come for?
CAROL: Have we got to talk in the corridor? (*A sudden
           thought hits her, peering into the flat*) Or is there
           someone with you …?
ALAN: Just the usual blonde, but she's probably climbing
           out of the bedroom window by now. Come along
           in!

*CAROL enters the hall. ALAN closes the front door. They
move into the living room.*

ALAN: Can I get you a drink?
CAROL: No, I haven't time. Harry's downstairs in the car,
           and he wants to catch the six-fifteen back to
           Town. (*She holds up the envelope*) I thought you
           might like to see this. It was at the office when I
           arrived. It's addressed to Mr Fielding.
ALAN: What is it?
CAROL: It's a photograph. (*She looks at the envelope*) It
           was posted in Lucerne on Tuesday; it should have
           arrived Friday morning.

*ALAN takes the envelope and opens it: he takes out a
postcard size photograph. It is a head and shoulders
photograph of BARBARA SMITH. Printed across the top of
the photograph are the words "Get Rid Of This Girl". ALAN
looks at CAROL, then at the envelope.*

CAROL: There was nothing with it – just the photograph.
ALAN nods and looks at the photograph again.
CAROL: What does that mean – "Get rid of this girl"?
ALAN: I don't know, Carol … Has anyone else seen this?
CAROL: No, I opened the envelope myself. When I saw
           what it was I thought you'd better see it straight
           away.

41

ALAN: And you didn't show it to anyone else?

CAROL: No. Well – no one at the office.

ALAN: What does that mean?

CAROL: I – I told Harry about it, naturally.

ALAN: And showed him the photograph?

CAROL: Er – yes.

ALAN puts the photograph down on the table, placing the envelope on top of it. He hesitates.

ALAN: Carol, tell me – how well did Harry know Tom Fielding?

CAROL: He hardly knew him at all. They met for the first time about ten days ago. It was on my birthday. We were having dinner at the Falstaff – Harry, Eric and I – and Mr Fielding came in with a party of friends. Naturally, I introduced Harry. But why are you interested in Harry? He's got nothing to do with this affair …

ALAN: Hasn't he, Carol? (*Suddenly: making a decision*) Look, I'm going to tell you something – something I shouldn't tell you. But I think, under the circumstances, I'm justified.

CAROL: If it's something you shouldn't tell me, Alan, then I would very much prefer …

ALAN: Carol, for God's sake! (*Takes her arm*) Now listen to me. Just before Barbara Smith died, she regained consciousness and kept asking for someone. A man called Harry Brent.

CAROL: Who – who told you this?

ALAN: Dr Fess – and the nurse. I've spoken to both of them.

CAROL: (*Bewildered*) I – I just don't believe it.

ALAN: It's true, Carol.

The doorbell rings. ALAN glances towards the hall.

ALAN: (*Quietly*) I've told you this in confidence; I don't
           want you to repeat it – not to anyone.

CAROL: Yes, but if Harry <u>did</u> know this girl, then surely …

ALAN: (*With authority*) Not to anyone – you understand?

CAROL looks at him, surprised by his tone.

CAROL: (*With a little nod, puzzled*) Yes, all right, Alan.

*ALAN turns and goes out into the hall. CAROL follows him.
ALAN opens the door. PHILIPS is standing outside.*

ALAN: Oh, hello, Roy! Come in!

PHILIPS is surprised to see CAROL.

PHILIPS: I – I hope I'm not interrupting anything?

ALAN: No, of course not. I was expecting you. Have you
           been to Dalesbury?

PHILIPS enters the hall.

PHILIPS: Yes, I've just got back.

ALAN: I think you know Carol?

PHILIPS: Yes, we've met before. Good evening, Miss
           Vyner.

CAROL: Good evening, Sergeant.

ALAN: (*To PHILIPS*) Go along inside, Roy – help
           yourself to a drink. I shan't be a minute.

PHILIPS: Thank you.

*PHILIPS gives a friendly nod to CAROL and goes into the
living room. ALAN holds open the front door for CAROL and
she hesitates.*

CAROL: There's no need to come down, Alan.

ALAN: I'll come down. (*With a suggestion of a smile*) I
           always used to.

*CAROL looks at him, then comes out into the corridor,
followed by ALAN. As they go, we see PHILIPS looking after
them as he takes his coat off.*

CUT TO: ALAN MILTON's flat. As before.

ALAN puts some soda in a glass of whisky and picks up his glass of milk. He carries both glasses across to PHILIPS who is standing by the table looking at the photograph of BARBARA SMITH. His hat and coat are on a nearby chair.

PHILIPS: Where did this come from?

ALAN: Carol brought it; it was sent to Fielding's. It arrived this morning. There was no letter with it – nothing. Just the photograph.

PHILIPS: (*Looking at the envelope*) Posted in Lucerne on the third …?

ALAN: Yes, it should have arrived Friday morning, the day he was killed. (*He moves down to PHILIPS*) But tell me about Dalesbury. What happened? Did you go to the theatre?

PHILIPS puts the photograph down.

PHILIPS: Yes, I did. The box office weren't particularly helpful I'm afraid. They seem to think it's possible – just possible – that both those tickets, Barbara Smith's and the one in the wallet, were bought by Jacqueline Dawson.

ALAN: Jacqueline Dawson?

PHILIPS: She's the star of the show; the guest artist. A month ago she was here, in Market Weldon, doing the same play. Before that she was in Southampton – week after next she's at Leatherhead.

ALAN: And she bought both tickets?

PHILIPS: (*A shrug*) The box office think she did, but they're not really sure. They're not really sure about anything. Miss Dawson has a large circle of friends and she likes to see them out in front whenever possible. To make sure of it she's always buying tickets and giving them away to people.

44

ALAN:	Did you see Miss Dawson?
PHILIPS:	No, she hadn't arrived when I left – besides, I thought I'd leave her to you. Sophisticated women aren't much in my line.
ALAN:	Is she very sophisticated?
PHILIPS:	(*Vaguely*) Well – you know what these actresses are.

The doorbell rings.

ALAN:	(*Thoughtfully*) You say she was here – in Market Weldon – about a month ago?
PHILIPS:	That's right – at 'The Playhouse'. My wife and I saw her. Damned boring play I thought, but she was pretty good. (*He nods towards the hall*) Are you expecting someone?

ALAN is still deep in thought: he suddenly realises what PHILIPS has said. He looks towards the hall.

ALAN:	Yes, I'm expecting a Mrs Tolly, she phoned me about ten minutes ago. She wants to talk to me about something.
PHILIPS:	Mrs Tolly? Is that the woman who used to run the canteen at Fielding's? Her husband has a stall in the market.
ALAN:	Yes, that's right. Do you know her?
PHILIP:	I've seen her about. I don't really know her.

The doorbell rings again and ALAN goes out into the hall. PHILIPS looks towards the hall, then down at the photograph and the envelope. He picks up the envelope again and studies it. We hear the opening and closing of the front door and the sound of voices. ALAN returns with Mrs Tolly. She stops dead when she sees PHILIPS.

MRS TOLLY:	(*To ALAN*) I didn't know there was goin't to be anyone else here.
ALAN:	That's all right, Mrs Tolly. This is a colleague of mine – Sergeant Philips.

PHILIPS: (*Pleasantly*) Good evening, Mrs Tolly.

ALAN: Do sit down, Mrs Tolly. Would you like a drink?

MRS TOLLY: Well – yes, I think I would. (*She sits on the settee*) Have you a gin and bitter lemon?

ALAN: Yes, I think so. A gin and tonic anyhow …

ALAN crosses to the drinks table.

MRS TOLLY: That'll do.   (*TO PHILIPS*) I really didn't know whether to come or not: but I talked it over with Harold, my husband, and he said, "Well, if I was you, Phyllis, I'd have a word with the Inspector about it. It might help, an' if it doesn't there's no harm done."

PHILIPS: It is about Mr Fielding that you …

MRS TOLLY: Yes, about the murder. I've been very upset about it, very upset.

PHILIPS: When did you leave Fielding's, Mrs Tolly?

MRS TOLLY: About six months ago. I was having trouble with my back – terrible trouble – and one day I said to myself, "Phyllis, you're a young woman still, and if you don't take things …" (*She breaks off and takes her drink from ALAN*) Oh, thanks. That's very nice of you. I can do with this, I must say. Cheers. (*Drinks*) We met last Christmas, didn't we? With your fian …. With Miss Vyner.

ALAN: That's right, at the staff party.

MRS TOLLY: That was quite a "do".

ALAN: Yes, it was – it was indeed. (*He sits on the arm of the settee*) Now what is it you want to see me about?

MRS TOLLY: I've talked to quite a lot of people about what happened on Friday. Friends of mine, at Fielding's, I mean. And I've read about the

46

murder, of course, read every blessed thing that's been written about it. (*She looks at ALAN and shakes her head*) But it just doesn't make sense, Mr Milton. It doesn't add up!

ALAN: What doesn't make sense?

MRS TOLLY: Well, everyone seems to think that the murder was a surprise – that poor old Fielding ... (*Suddenly*) Mr Milton, he knew he was going to be murdered! He'd been warned about it – he knew it was on the cards!

ALAN looks across at PHILIPS: rises and moves towards MRS TOLLY.

ALAN: Mr Fielding <u>knew</u> he was going to be murdered?

MRS TOLLY: Yes, he did. He'd been warned – he was told to be careful, to be on the lookout ...

PHILIPS: But who warned him, Mrs Tolly?

ALAN: (*To PHILIPS*) Wait a minute, Roy! (*To MRS TOLLY*) Start at the beginning – let's have the whole story, right from the beginning.

MRS TOLLY: I have a sister – a widow – she lives the other side of London and once a month I pop over there with something or other ... She's got three kids and her husband only left two hundred quid, so she doesn't exactly run from one party to another. Anyway, I was over there four weeks ago – four weeks yesterday to be precise – and I missed the last flipping bus home. I was livid. Still, there was nothing I could do about it. I just had to walk to the tube and catch a train from Waterloo...

47

As Mrs Tolly is talking, we CUT TO: A London Street at night.

MRS TOLLY is walking along a busy street in a London suburb. She looks tired and exhausted, and is carrying a string shopping bag as well as a handbag.

MRS TOLLY's VOICE: … I'd been walking about twenty minutes or so when I saw a café on the other side of the road. I was hot and tired, my back was killing me, and I felt awful. I knew if I didn't 'ave a cup of tea I'd never make Marble Arch, let alone Market Weldon.

MRS TOLLY crosses the road and goes into the café.

CUT TO: The Como Café: near Edgware Road.

It is an Italian style coffee bar with several partitioned tables and alcoves: most of the tables face a long counter complete with stools and the inevitable espresso machine.

There are one or two people in the café but business is not brisk. MRS TOLLY enters, and crosses to one of the alcoves: she puts down her things, makes herself comfortable, then opens her handbag and with a sigh of relief takes out a packet of cigarettes. MARIO – a white coated waiter – comes from behind the bar and joins MRS TOLLY who is taking stock of her   surroundings as MARIO speaks.

MARIO: Good evening! What would you like?

MRS TOLLY: I'd like a nice pot of tea, please.

MARIO: I'm afraid we don't usually serve tea; most of our customers drink coffee…

MRS TOLLY: All right, love, coffee – plenty of sugar.

MARIO: It's on the table.

MARIO returns to the counter. MRS TOLLY searches her handbag for her lighter, then notices the book-matches on the table. She is lighting her cigarette when HARRY BRENT suddenly enters from the street. He wears a camel-hair coat and looks tense and worried as he stands staring at the counter. After a moment he walks past MRS TOLLY to the next table which is partly hidden by a partition. MRS TOLLY glances at HARRY but it is obvious that she is disinterested in him and has never seen him before. As HARRY reaches the table the man rises from behind the partition and we recognise him as THOMAS FIELDING. He is obviously relieved to see HARRY BRENT.

THOMAS: Harry – you made it!

HARRY: Hello, Tom! (*Shaking hands*) I'm sorry I'm so late. I hope you haven't been waiting long?

THOMAS: No. No, that's all right. I was hungry so I had something to eat. Sit down, Harry.

HARRY: Tom, I can't stay, I'm in a mad hurry as usual. (*Glancing at his watch*) I'm seeing Jacqueline at eleven o'clock.

To her surprise MRS TOLLY has recognised TOM FIELDING's voice and she quickly turns her head and looks up at the partition. The two men are taking their seats at the table now, unaware of her presence.

CUT TO: TOM FIELDING's table.

THOMAS is sitting with the partition behind him. HARRY BRENT sits facing him. There are the remains of a meal on the table. MRS TOLLY is on the other side of the partition, out of view.

THOMAS: And how is our Miss Dawson?

HARRY: She's all right, but she's worried, Tom.

THOMAS: About me?

HARRY: Of course. Who else? (*Quietly, leaning forward*) Tom, you know the last time we met – you remember what we talked about?

THOMAS: (*Smiling*) I do. I do indeed. The usual topic.

HARRY: Tom, I hope you've changed your mind.

49

THOMAS: No, I'm sorry, Harry. I haven't. Look – I've thought about this. I know precisely what I'm doing. Now, please, don't interfere, there's a good chap!

HARRY: (*Anxiously*) But do you know what you're doing, Tom? Do you <u>really</u> know?

THOMAS: I've taken risks before, this isn't the first time.

HARRY: This is different; you know damn well it's different!

THOMAS: (*Shaking his head*) I'm not changing my mind, Harry.

HARRY: When I told your friends about it – do you know what they said?

THOMAS: No – what did they say?

HARRY: (*Quietly*) You're not going to like this, Tom.

THOMAS: Go ahead – tell me. What did they say?

HARRY pauses.

HARRY: They said: Tell Tom Fielding if he goes through with this it's a hundred to one, he'll be murdered.

There is a long pause: FIELDING gives a little nod.

THOMAS: (*Resigned*) Well – that's a risk I've got to take.

HARRY: But you <u>haven't</u> got to take it! That's just the point – you haven't got to take it!

THOMAS: I'm sorry, Harry, but I'm not changing my mind. (*He pats HARRY's arm*) Now please don't worry – and tell Jacqueline Dawson to relax. If I'm in difficulty I'll contact her, I promise you.

HARRY looks at FIELDING and hesitates.

HARRY: That's your last word?

THOMAS: My last word.

HARRY rises.

HARRY: (*Pleasantly*) Well, all I can say is – you really are an obstinate old bastard …

THOMAS: (*Smiling*) Yes, Harry, I really am.

CUT TO: *MARIO who is leaving the counter with a pot of tea etc on a tray. He crosses to MRS TOLLY's table. She is smoking her cigarette: she looks puzzled: confused. It is obvious that she has overheard the conversation between HARRY BRENT and TOM FIELDING. MARIO puts the tea things on the table. He is pleased with himself for having produced tea instead of coffee.*

MARIO: Pot of tea …

MRS TOLLY stares at him.

MRS TOLLY: What?

MARIO: Tea.

MRS TOLLY: Oh … oh, ta. (*Pulling herself together*) Thanks, love …

MARIO looks at her, obviously disappointed by her reaction and returns to the counter. MRS TOLLY slowly pours herself a cup of tea. HARRY BRENT appears from behind the partition, walking past MRS TOLLY's table towards the door. She stares after him, then thoughtfully drinks her tea. After a little while TOM FIELDING rises from his table and crosses over to the counter to pay for his meal. MRS TOLLY is aware of the fact that he has moved, and half turns her back towards the counter in the hope that she won't be noticed. TOM receives his change from MARIO, turns, and then for the first time sees MRS TOLLY. After a momentary hesitation he crosses to her table.

THOMAS: Why, hello, Mrs Tolly! This is a surprise!

MRS TOLLY: Good – good evening, Mr Fielding.

MRS TOLLY half rises.

THOMAS: No, no, don't get up, please! (*He sits down at the table*) I certainly didn't expect to see you in this part of the world.

MRS TOLLY: (*Ill at ease*) I've – I've been over to my sister's for the day. I usually pop over about once a month if I can manage it.

51

THOMAS: Oh, I see. Is that the one whose husband died about six months ago?

MRS TOLLY: Yes. Yes, that's right. I've only got the one sister.

THOMAS: And now you're on your way home?

MRS TOLLY: Yes, I'm catching the eleven-fifty from Waterloo. Missed the Green Line, I'm afraid.

THOMAS: Well, don't worry. I can give you a lift.

MRS TOLLY: (*Brightening up*) Oh – thanks. Thanks a lot.

MRS TOLLY starts to collect her things.

MRS TOLLY: That'll be a great help.

THOMAS: No, no, finish your tea – there's no hurry. (*Pleasantly; smiling at her*) As a matter of fact I think I'll have another cup of coffee.

TOM turns and calls MARIO to the counter.

THOMAS: Bring me another coffee, will you, please?

TOM FIELDING continues to smile at MRS TOLLY. His manner is friendly and relaxed. He appears completely unaware of the fact that she might have overheard his conversation with HARRY BRENT. He takes out his pipe and tobacco pouch.

MRS TOLLY's VOICE: He didn't seem a bit perturbed or worried about anything. He just sat there, smiling. I don't think he even realised I'd been listening to his conversation. If he did, it certainly didn't bother him at all …

CUT TO: The living room of ALAN MILTON's flat. As before.

ALAN and PHILIPS are listening to MRS TOLLY as she tells her story.

MRS TOLLY: … On the way home we talked about all sorts of things. The cost of living – running the canteen … how he'd had a spot of bother with

	the local Council. He was ever so nice, ever so friendly, it was just like old times in fact. But he never referred to his conversation with the other man. And neither did I, of course.
ALAN:	And you say all this took place exactly four weeks ago?
MRS TOLLY:	Yes, four weeks yesterday to be precise.
PHILIPS:	Did you tell anyone about it – discuss it with anyone?
MRS TOLLY:	Only Harold – my husband.
ALAN:	And what did he say?
MRS TOLLY:	He didn't believe me. He said I'd imagined it, or hadn't heard the conversation properly. I began to think he was right. Then of course when the murder happened we – we both got into a right old tiz.
PHILIPS:	You did the correct thing when you phoned the Inspector. No doubt about that, Mrs Tolly.
MRS TOLLY:	Well, I hope so, sir.
ALAN:	Mrs Tolly – you're quite sure the name Dawson was mentioned – Jacqueline Dawson?
MRS TOLLY:	Oh, yes, I'm quite sure. I recognised it immediately. She's an actress, isn't she?

ALAN rises.

ALAN:	Yes, that's right, Mrs Tolly. She's an actress. (*He looks at MRS TOLLY; quietly*) Now tell me more about the other man – the man called Harry.
MRS TOLLY:	He was about thirty-two or three. Tall, dark, crinkly hair. Good looking, I suppose.
ALAN:	Had you ever seen him before?
MRS TOLLY:	No, never.
ALAN:	And you haven't seen him since?

MRS TOLLY: (*Shaking her head*) No, I haven't.

PHILIPS: What was he wearing, Mrs Tolly?

MRS TOLLY: He had a light-coloured coat – camel-hair, I think you call it. He didn't seem to have a hat, at least he wasn't wearing one.

ALAN: Is there anything else you can remember about him?

MRS TOLLY: No, I don't think there is. He had a pleasant sort of voice, but it's a bit difficult to describe a voice to anyone, isn't it?

ALAN: (*Facing Mrs Tolly*) Would you recognise him again if you saw him?

MRS TOLLY: Yes …

ALAN: You're sure, Mrs Tolly?

MRS TOLLY: Yes, I'm quite sure. (*Very confident*) Oh, I'd recognise him all right.

CUT TO: JACQUELINE DAWSON's dressing room at the Dalesbury Repertory Theatre.

The evening performance is over, and JACQUELINE DAWSON is sitting in front of her mirror removing the last traces of her stage makeup. She has taken off her costume and is wearing a dressing gown. JACQUELINE is an attractive, if somewhat determined looking, woman in her thirties. There is an armchair in the dressing room and an ornate screen stands at right angles to a corner cupboard which contains JACQUELINE's clothes. There is a knock on the door and TONY MOORE enters. Apart from being the leading man TONY runs the repertory company.

JACQUELINE: What is it, Tony?

TONY: Sorry, darling. There's a character out here says he's Detective-Inspector Milton and he'd like to have a word with you.

JACQUELINE: Detective-Inspector Milton?

TONY: Yes, sweetie. He doesn't look like a police
               Inspector. Not the ones I've played.

JACQUELINE: All right, Tony. Ask him to come in.

TONY goes out into the corridor. JACQUELINE thoughtfully
picks up a cigarette carton off the table, discovers it is empty,
and drops it back amongst the make-up paraphernalia. ALAN
appears in the doorway; he is carrying his hat and coat and
the envelope containing the photograph of BARBARA SMITH.

ALAN: May I come in?

JACQUELINE: Yes, please do.

ALAN enters the room, closing the door behind him.

ALAN: It's very good of you to see me, Miss
               Dawson. I must apologise for disturbing
               you.

JACQUELINE: That's all right. I'm curious. (*Crossing over*
               to the cupboard) I knew the audience were
               hostile, but I didn't think they'd send for the
               police.

ALAN: (*Smiling*) I'm investigating a murder case
               and I think you might be able to help me.

JACQUELINE takes a dress from the cupboard and carefully
closes the door.

JACQUELINE: A murder case, did you say?

ALAN: Yes; I expect you know the case I'm
               referring to.

JACQUELINE: No, I'm afraid I don't.

ALAN: (*Watching her*) Tom Fielding.

JACQUELINE: Tom Fielding? Who's Tom Fielding?

ALAN: Wasn't he a friend of yours?

JACQUELINE looks at ALAN.

JACQUELINE: No, I'm sorry, he wasn't. (*Suddenly*) Wait a
               minute! Is that the Market Weldon affair?
               He was shot by some girl or other?

55

ALAN: Yes, that's right. A Miss Smith – Barbara Smith.

JACQUELINE: Yes, well I'm afraid I'd never heard of Mr Fielding, or Barbara Smith either for that matter – not until I read about them. Was the old boy having an affair with her?

ALAN: I don't think so.

JACQUELINE: Well, that's the usual story, isn't it? (*She indicates the screen*) Look, Inspector, do you mind if I get dressed? I'm supposed to be going to a party.

ALAN: No, of course not. Go ahead.

JACQUELINE turns towards the table, picks up the empty cigarette carton again, opens it, then tosses it down. ALAN takes a packet of cigarettes out of his pocket

ALAN: Would you like a cigarette?

JACQUELINE: (*Smiling at him*) Oh, thank you. That's very sweet of you.

JACQUELINE takes the packet of cigarettes from ALAN and goes behind the screen. ALAN sits on the arm of the chair facing the screen.

ALAN: When we arrested Barbara Smith, we found a theatre ticket in her handbag. It was for your play, Miss Dawson – next Saturday's performance. We made inquiries about the ticket; apparently it was one you bought.

JACQUELINE: (*Slipping on her dress*) One I bought?

ALAN: Yes.

JACQUELINE: But that's not possible, unless of course she ... (*Hesitates*)

ALAN: Go on, Miss Dawson.

JACQUELINE: Well, to be truthful, Inspector, whenever I find myself playing a God-forsaken town

	like this I always buy a certain number of tickets and give them away. But they're usually given to people I know, or have met at some time or other.
ALAN:	(*Pleasantly*) Well p-perhaps you're mistaken. Perhaps you've met Miss Smith?
JACQUELINE:	Barbara Smith? It's a common enough name, but – I certainly can't place her.
ALAN:	(*Watching the screen; casually*) Maybe you met her at a party – or with a friend of yours? Mr Brent, perhaps?
JACQUELINE:	(*After a moment*) Brent?
ALAN:	Yes, Harry Brent. He is a friend of yours, isn't he?

There is a long pause. ALAN is puzzled by the silence.

ALAN: Did you hear what I said, Miss Dawson?

The silence continues. Puzzled, ALAN rises, and is about to move towards the screen when JACQUELINE emerges, having now changed into her dress. She is lighting a cigarette.

JACQUELINE: Yes, I heard you. (*Curtly*) I'm sorry, I don't know anyone called Harry Brent.

JACQUELINE tosses the packet of cigarettes to ALAN and as he puts them in his pocket she moves to the table and the make-up mirror. Her manner is suddenly off-hand, almost rude. ALAN hesitates, then takes the photograph out of the envelope and puts it down in front of her.

ALAN: That's a photograph of Barbara Smith.

JACQUELINE is busy with her hair, she barely glances at the photograph.

JACQUELINE: Yes, I know. I've seen it. It was in the papers.

ALAN: Not this one.

ALAN is looking at JACQUELINE, faintly surprised by her change of manner. There is a pause.

JACQUELINE: (*Obviously dismissing him*) I'm sorry, I'm afraid I can't help you. (*Ignoring ALAN and calling to TONY in the next dressing room*) Darling, are you nearly ready?

TONY's VOICE: (*From the next dressing room*) Coming, sweetie!

After a moment, and with his eyes still on JACQUELINE, ALAN picks up the photograph.

CUT TO: ALAN MILTON's flat.

ALAN enters the hall, he stops, puzzled to find the light on. He takes off his hat and coat, hangs them up, puts down the envelope, and then walks through into the living room. He puts the light on there and turns towards the drinks table: just before he reaches the table he stops dead – suddenly sensing someone else in the room besides himself. ALAN swings round. A thick-set, fastidiously dressed little man is sitting in the armchair. He has a gun in his hand and is watching ALAN. His name is KEVIN JASON and he hails from Belfast.

ALAN: Who are you? What are you doing here?

JASON: It's taken you a devil of a time to get from Dalesbury, Mr Milton. (*Rising*) What did you do – walk?

ALAN goes towards the phone.

JASON: Don't touch that phone! If you touch it I'll blow your hand off.

ALAN hesitates.

ALAN: Who are you and what do you want?

JASON: Unless I've been badly informed, dear boy, I think you have a packet of cigarettes on you.

ALAN: (*Puzzled*) Cigarettes?

58

JASON: Yes. Cigarettes; "fags" if you prefer a more proletarian phraseology. Anyway, that's what I want. (*Smiling*) That's all. Just the packet of cigarettes.

ALAN: What is this – some kind of a joke?

JASON: No, it's not a joke. (*He moves towards ALAN*) You'll soon find that out if you're daft enough to try and take advantage of me. (*Quickly, as ALAN puts his hand in his pocket*) Now don't move, dear boy! Don't be stupid!

ALAN: (*Still with his hand in his pocket*) I thought you wanted the cigarettes?

JASON: Take them out of your pocket and throw them onto that table.

ALAN hesitates, then slowly takes the cigarettes out of his pocket and looks at the packet.

JASON: (*Angrily*) I told you to throw them onto the table!

ALAN ignores Jason and still stares at the packet of cigarettes. We see that someone has scrawled a message across the packet with a ballpoint pen.

JASON: You heard what I said!

ALAN slowly looks up at JASON.

ALAN: Now I understand. I'm catching on. (*He looks at the cigarettes again*) I get the message.

JASON: (*Quietly*) What did Jacqueline Dawson write? What did she put on the cigarettes?

ALAN hesitates, then looks at the cigarettes as if about to read the message.

JASON: Go on – read it!

As JASON speaks ALAN quickly throws the packet of cigarettes onto the drinks table; taken by surprise JASON takes his eyes off ALAN to follow the flight of the cigarettes and at that precise moment ALAN springs forward and knocks the gun out of JASON's hand. JASON quickly recovers and

59

makes an immediate attempt to retrieve the gun – but ALAN hits out, knocking the Irishman off balance. ALAN turns, searching the floor with his eyes – looking for the gun. He suddenly sees it. JASON realises what is happening and decides to escape – he rushes across the room and out into the hall. As ALAN picks up the gun, we hear the slamming of the front door. ALAN looks towards the hall, hesitates, then finally decides not to pursue JASON. He moves to the drinks table and picks up the packet of cigarettes. ALAN looks at the message again and we see that it says: "Can't talk now. Suggest you visit Flat 18, Kingsdown Mansions, Richmond.")

CUT TO: A Road near the river in Richmond, Surrey. After midnight.
An E-type Jaguar draws to a standstill at the side of the road. In the background, across a terraced lawn of shrubs and bushes, we can see the outline of a large block of "luxury" flats. HARRY BRENT gets out of the car and, after glancing up and down the road, switches off the car lights and closes the door. He wears the camelhair overcoat; as he walks away from the car he glances at his watch.

CUT TO: The Main Entrance to Kingsdown Mansions.
A light suddenly comes on and REG BRYER appears in the porch entrance to the flats. We see the name "Kingsdown Mansions" over the entrance door. Reg is the head porter; a retired military man in his early fifties. He wears a dressing-gown over grey flannel trousers and an open neck shirt. He peers somewhat shortsightedly, across the lawn, then turns and calls to someone inside the hall.

REG: I told you – the confounded thing isn't out there!
Reg turns and goes back into the building. After a moment the porch light is extinguished. HARRY emerges from the shadows and – with his eyes on the porch – quickly crosses

the lawn towards the tradesmen's entrance at the side of the building. When he reaches the side entrance he stops for a moment in the doorway. He makes sure he is not being watched, then takes a pair of gloves out of his overcoat pocket and puts them on. He carefully adjusts the gloves as he goes into the building.

CUT TO: Entrance Hall of Kingsdown Mansions. There is a lift in the centre of the hall with an "Out of Order" sign on it; a carpeted staircase continues from the basement to the first floor.

REG slowly comes up from the basement carrying a large black cat. He speaks to it.

REG: … I've been looking all over the place for you! You're a confounded nuisance, Blackie! There's no other way to describe you – just a confounded nuisance. (*He strokes the cat*) If I had any sense I'd tie a brick round your wretched neck and toss you into the river.

ALAN enters from the porch. REG stops, and stares at him obviously surprised to see a visitor at this hour of the morning.

ALAN: Excuse me – is this Kingsdown Mansions?

REG: That's right. I'm the Head Porter – can I help you?

ALAN: I'm looking for flat 18 …

REG: First floor – at the end of the corridor.

ALAN: Thank you.

ALAN goes up the staircase, watched by REG.

CUT TO: Outside the Front Door of Flat 18.

ALAN arrives and presses the doorbell. There is no reply. He waits a moment and then presses the bell again. There is a pause. ALAN is about to press the bell for a third time when a woman's voice, from a distant part of the flat, can be heard calling, "Wait a minute – I'm coming!" ALAN waits. Suddenly, from within the flat, the woman's voice can be heard raised in a terrified scream. The scream is followed by the immediate sound of a prolonged struggle, further screams – then silence. ALAN has already reacted to the first scream for help and is throwing his weight against the door in an attempt to break it open. REG BRYER comes running along the corridor.

REG: For God's sake, what's happened? What's going on?

ALAN: Have you got a key to this door?

REG feels in his trousers pocket.

REG: Yes, I – I think so …

ALAN: Then get the door open – quickly man!

Flustered and trembling, Reg searches his clothes for the key.

CUT TO: The Drawing Room of Flat 18, Kingsdown Mansions. This is a fussy, feminine room; rather over-furnished. There are a number of prints on the walls – most of them in pretty bad taste. There is an alcove – leading to the hall – and several doors to bedrooms, bathroom, kitchen, etc. It is obvious that a struggle has recently taken place in the room; chairs and tables are overturned, books and cushions scattered all over the place.

The body of a woman is slumped across the corner of the settee; her dress badly torn; a large cushion over her face. ALAN rushes in from the hall followed by REG BRYER. They stop dead; staring at the woman. ALAN quickly crosses to the settee and removes the cushion; at the same time kneeling down as he examines the body. REG stands watching, tense and frightened. From outside comes the sound of a car making a quick getaway. ALAN hears the noise of the car and rises, as he does so REG BRYER moves towards the settee.

ALAN: She's dead…

REG stares at the woman on the settee. ALAN removes the cushion from her face and we see that it is MRS TOLLY.

ALAN: Her name's Tolly. Have you seen her before?

END OF EPISODE TWO

.

EPISODE THREE

THE PEN

OPEN TO: The Drawing Room of Flat 18, Kingsdown Mansions.

ALAN MILTON and REG BRYER are standing over the dead body of MRS TOLLY.

ALAN: Her name's Tolly. Have you seen her before?

Reg stares at ALAN in obvious surprise.

REG: Of course I've seen her before! And her name isn't Tolly, it's Stafford – Phyllis Stafford.

ALAN: Phyllis Stafford?

REG: Yes, she lives here – she's the tenant. (*Curious*) Look, who are you – who is it you wanted to see?

ALAN takes a handkerchief out of his pocket, covers his hand with it, and crosses down to the telephone.

ALAN: My name's Milton. I'm a police Inspector. I was under the impression a Miss Dawson lived here – Jacqueline Dawson.

REG shakes his head: bewildered.

REG: I've never heard of Miss Dawson! She hasn't got a flat here, not in Kingsdown Mansions …

ALAN nods, picks up the phone, then takes a pen from his inside pocket and starts to dial 999 with it.

CUT TO: ALAN MILTON's Office.

ALAN is sitting behind his desk interviewing HAROLD TOLLY. TOLLY, a tall, heavily built man in his late thirties, wears a check suit with a flower in the buttonhole. MR TOLLY is fond of buttonholes; he is also fond of the silver identity bracelet he wears. Normally a self-possessed individual it would appear that he has been badly shaken by the news of his wife's murder.

ALAN: … Mr Tolly, I realise this has been a terrible shock for you …

TOLLY: My God, you can say that again!

ALAN: But you must try and help us. You must be absolutely frank about everything, otherwise …

TOLLY: But I am being frank about everything! I've told you … I didn't know my wife was using her maiden name. I didn't know she had a flat in Richmond. (*He rises and paces up and down*) I travel about a great deal. I'm all over the place. I've got a couple of stalls here, in the market – one at Dalesbury, another one at Kingston, and I've just opened a little place at Byfleet.

ALAN: Yes, I know, Mr Tolly.

TOLLY: Naturally, with travelling about like that I … I … Look, I'm not trying to conceal anything, Inspector. There's no reason why I should for God's sake. Phyllis and I lived together; we shared a cottage together, but … Well, we both had our own friends and … and we did exactly what we liked.

ALAN: I see.

TOLLY: I can't be franker than that, now can I, Inspector?

ALAN: It would be difficult, Mr Tolly. Now would you mind telling me where you were last night and what you were doing?

TOLLY: Last night? I was at the Byfleet place until eleven o'clock going through the accounts. I suppose I got home about a quarter to twelve.

ALAN: (*Nodding*) Thank you. Now if you don't mind …

TOLLY: (*Interrupting him*) Now if you don't mind, I'd like to ask you a few questions for a change.

ALAN: Go ahead.

TOLLY: I understand it was you that went to the flat last night – it was you in fact that discovered Phyllis.

ALAN: Yes, it was.

68

TOLLY: Well – how did that happen? Was my wife a friend of yours then?

ALAN looks at TOLLY, faintly surprised by the question.

ALAN: (*Quietly*) No, I'd only met her twice before.

ROY PHILIPS bursts in from the general office: he wears outdoor clothes and carries a man's sports jacket over his arm. It is obvious that he has some important information he wishes to impart.

PHILIPS: Oh, I'm sorry, sir. I didn't realise you had someone with you.

ALAN: That's all right. Mr Tolly … Sergeant Philips.

PHILIPS nods to TOLLY.

ALAN: Sit down, Roy.

PHILIPS sits on the arm of the chair.

ALAN: (*To TOLLY*) I went to the flat because I thought a Miss Dawson – Jacqueline Dawson – lived there.

TOLLY: Jacqueline Dawson? The actress?

ALAN: Yes. Do you know Miss Dawson?

TOLLY: No, but I've seen her on the stage, of course. Seen her several times.

ALAN nods and rises from the desk. He deliberately changes the subject.

ALAN: Mr Tolly, four weeks ago – four weeks last Sunday to be precise – your wife went up to London to see her sister. On the way home she called into a coffee bar and accidentally overheard a conversation between Mr Fielding and a friend of his. Now when Mrs Tolly first told you about this, did she say whether …

TOLLY: (*Interrupting him*) Wait a minute! Fielding? You mean Tom Fielding – the man she used to work for?

ALAN: Yes. (*Looks at TOLLY*) But you know about this incident. Your wife discussed it with you.

TOLLY: What incident? What exactly is she supposed to have discussed with me?

ALAN: Didn't your wife tell you that she'd overheard a conversation between Mr Fielding and a man called Harry? Didn't she tell you …

TOLLY: (*Shaking his head*) No! I don't know anything about this. She went to see her sister – she was always popping up to Town to see her. But she never said anything to me about a coffee bar, or Tom Fielding, or someone called Harry. (*Irritated*) I don't get this.

ALAN looks at TOLLY, then suddenly, after a long pause, holds out his hand.

ALAN: All right, sir. Don't worry about it. It's nothing. I've obviously made a mistake.

ALAN and TOLLY shake hands.

ALAN: If we should want to get in touch with you during the next few days, where will you be, Mr Tolly?

TOLLY: Well, I shall be here tomorrow – it's market day. The rest of the week I shall probably be at Byfleet. (*Shaking his head*) Although, God knows, I don't feel like doing any work at the moment.

ALAN takes TOLLY to the door.

ALAN: If there's anything we can do – anything to help you – just let us know. You can always talk to Sergeant Philips if I'm not here.

TOLLY: Thank you.

PHILIPS: Goodbye, Mr Tolly.

TOLLY turns, nods to PHILIPS, then follows ALAN into the outer office. PHILIPS rises and moves to the desk. ALAN returns.

PHILIPS: Was he telling the truth?

ALAN: (*Thoughtfully*) About Fielding? Yes, I think he was. I think Mrs Tolly lied to us, Roy. I don't

think she told him a thing about the coffee bar
incident.

PHILIPS: If it ever happened.

ALAN: Well, if it didn't happen – then why did she invent
the story?

PHILIPS: (*Shaking his head*) I don't know. I just don't
know.

ALAN: Anyway, what happened this morning? You've
obviously got some news. I hope it's good.

PHILIPS: Well, it's certainly interesting. I finally tracked
down Miss Dawson. She has a flat at Esher. She
claims that she didn't write anything on the
cigarette packet, she says she's never heard of a
Mrs Tolly and she's certainly never been to
Kingsdown Mansions.

ALAN: M'm. Go on …

PHILIPS: After seeing our friend Jacqueline, I drove out to
Richmond and went through Mrs Tolly's flat
again.

PHILIPS picks up the sports jacket.

PHILIPS: I found this in one of the airing cupboards.

ALAN: Whose is it?

PHILIPS: There's no name in it, except for the tailor's. But
there's a reference number, so I rang the tailor
straight away and …

ALAN: (*Impatient*) Roy, who does it belong to? Whose is
it?

PHILIPS hesitates, then looks at ALAN.

PHILIPS: It's Eric Vyner's.

CUT TO: A ploughed field.

*ERIC and TOM, a mechanic, are by a tractor which
resolutely refuses to start. TOM is 'tinkering' with the*

carburettor as he swings the starting handle, but all to no avail.

ERIC: You'll just have to leave it, Tom, and get in touch with the garage.

TOM: But I don't understand it, Guv'nor. I just don't understand it – she went like a bird all day yesterday.

ALAN is walking across the ploughed field towards the two men. He is carrying the sports jacket. TOM continues to tinker with the tractor. ERIC turns and to his surprise sees ALAN walking towards him. He goes to meet him)

ERIC: Hello, Alan! What are you doing up so early? I thought you boys didn't start work until ten o'clock?

ALAN: You've obviously been misinformed, Eric – and it's not ten anyway, it's a quarter to eleven.

ERIC: *(Surprised)* What? Is it really? *(He looks at his watch)* Good Lord! How time flies! We don't seem to have done a blessed thing this morning.

ALAN: I won't keep you a minute, Eric. I just wanted to know if you'd seen this jacket before?

ERIC: *(Looking at the jacket)* Why, yes! It's mine. *(He touches it)* It's the one I lent Harry.

ALAN: Harry Brent?

ERIC: Yes.

ALAN: When did you lend it to him?

ERIC: Oh, about three weeks ago. He came down for the weekend and we went fishing together. It rained cats and dogs; the pair of us got drenched so I lent him that jacket. It's an old one of mine. Harry took it back to Town with him. As a matter of fact I'd forgotten all about it.

ALAN: I see.

ERIC: (*Curious*) But what are you doing with it? Where did you get it from?

ALAN: It – it was brought into my office this morning. Eric, does the name Stafford – Phyllis Stafford – mean anything to you?

ERIC: Phyllis Stafford? (*Thoughtfully*) No, I don't think so.

ALAN: What about Tolly? Mrs Tolly?

ERIC: Yes, I've heard of Mrs Tolly, of course. She used to work at Fielding's.

ALAN: (*Nodding*) Stafford's her maiden name, or rather it was.

ERIC: Oh – I didn't know that. (*Puzzled; a sudden thought*) What do you mean – it was?

ALAN: (*Ignoring the question*) How well did you know Mrs Tolly, Eric? Was she a friend of yours?

ERIC: Good heavens, no! I don't suppose I've said half a dozen words to her. But look here, Alan, you're talking about the woman as if she's dead!

ALAN: (*Looking at ERIC*) She is dead – she was murdered, strangled. We found her body last night, in a flat at Richmond.

ERIC: Good God …

During this conversation TOM has been "swinging" the tractor in a last desperate attempt to get it started; suddenly the machine roars into life. ERIC turns, taken by surprise.

TOM: (*Beaming*) I knew darn well she'd start … Temperamental hussy …

ALAN touches ERIC's arm.

ALAN: I've got an appointment, I'll tell you about the coat later.

ERIC: (*Turning back to ALAN*) No – no, tell me now, Alan.

ALAN: Later, Eric …

ALAN nods and quickly makes his way back across the field. ERIC stands watching him, obviously puzzled.

CUT TO: THOMAS FIELDING's Office.

CAROL is frantically busy sorting out various invoices, checking estimates, and dealing with a hundred and one routine matters. The office seems to reflect a little of the confusion which has suddenly descended on the firm with the death of Tom Fielding. GEORGE LONGFIELD enters from the outer office. He is a senior clerk; a pleasant man in his late twenties. He carries a file of correspondence.

GEORGE: I'm sorry, Carol, I can't find that letter. I've looked everywhere.

CAROL: Oh dear! Have you had a word with Dora?

GEORGE: No, not yet. I didn't want to bother her.

CAROL: (*Good naturedly*) Well bother her, George! Bother her – but don't bother me!

GEORGE: (*Smiling*) Yes, all right, Carol. By the way, Mr Fielding's housekeeper wants to see you. She phoned me last night just after you left.

CAROL: Mrs Green?

GEORGE: Yes.

CAROL: What does she want, do you know?

The telephone starts to ring.

GEORGE: I don't know; she's going to ring this morning some time.

CAROL picks up the telephone receiver and GEORGE puts the papers he is carrying on the desk.

CAROL: (*On phone*)

During this next conversation we cut back and forth between CAROL in THOMAS FIELDING's office and MOLLIE GREEN who is in a telephone box.

MRS GREEN: Can I speak to Miss Vyner, please?

CAROL: This is Miss Vyner – who is that?

MRS GREEN: Oh, good morning, Miss Vyner. This is Mrs Green, Mr Fielding's housekeeper …

CAROL: Oh, hello, Mrs Green. I'm sorry I was out when you phoned last night. What can I do for you?

MRS GREEN: I'm leaving for Canada next week and I was wondering if …

CAROL: (*Surprised*) Canada?

MRS GREEN: Yes, I've got a married daughter out there. She and her husband emigrated just over four years ago.

CAROL: Yes, of course. I remember now!

MRS GREEN: Miss Vyner, I hope you don't think this is a bit presume … cheeky of me, but – last Christmas I gave Mr Fielding a pen, a fountain pen I mean, for a Christmas box …

CAROL: Yes, I remember. It's here now – in front of me.

MRS GREEN: Well, I wondered if – if I could have it back? I know it's a bit of a cheek … But you see, I've got to take Bert – my son-in-law – a present and … Well, the pen isn't much use to Mr Fielding now, is it, Duckie?

CAROL: (*Smiling*) Well – I don't see why you shouldn't have it back, Mrs Green. Just pop in one morning and I'll give it to you.

MRS GREEN: Thank you, Miss Vyner. I'll drop in about twelve o'clock, if that's convenient?

CAROL: This morning? Yes – all right, twelve o'clock.

CAROL replaces the receiver, looks at GEORGE, and is about to pick up the pen when HARRY BRENT appears in the doorway: he wears the same overcoat he wore on his visit to Kingsdown Mansions.

HARRY: May I come in?

75

CAROL: (*Surprised*) Harry! (*Going over to him*) Darling, what on earth are you doing here?

HARRY: I thought perhaps you could use some help this morning.

CAROL: You can say that again!

GEORGE returns to the outer office.

HARRY: (*Holding CAROL and kissing her*) How are you, Carol? How are you feeling?

CAROL: Oh, I'm all right. I feel much better now.

They move away from each other.

HARRY: You looked pretty rotten last night. I was worried about you. Very worried.

CAROL: Is that why you came down this morning?

HARRY: Well – (*Smiling*) – I'm on my way to Guildford; I've got an appointment there at half past twelve.

CAROL: You could have gone via Scotland.

HARRY: I've got the car; it'll only take me about forty-five minutes from here.

HARRY turns towards the desk; not looking at CAROL.

HARRY: Carol, there's something I want to ask you. I've been thinking about it ever since you dropped me at the station last night.

CAROL: Well?

HARRY is still turned away from CAROL.

CAROL: What is it, Harry?

HARRY: (*Quietly: facing her*) What did Alan Milton say to you when you gave him the photograph?

CAROL: I told you. He – he just thanked me for taking it along, that's all.

HARRY: You were with him for about fifteen minutes afterwards, on the way to the station, you looked desperately unhappy and you hardly said a word. It's my opinion he told you something last night – something about me.

76

CAROL: (*Faintly embarrassed*) No, Harry …

HARRY: If he did, I think it's only fair that you should tell me what it was.

CAROL: (*Moving away from him*) You were hardly mentioned. We were discussing the photograph the whole time. Then Sergeant Philips turned up and …

HARRY: Go on …

CAROL: (*"On edge"*) There's nothing to go on about – then I came down to the car and we drove to the station.

There is a long pause. HARRY is looking at her.

HARRY: Carol, I'm sorry – I'm very sorry – but I just don't believe you.

CAROL: (*Suddenly; almost turning on him*) All right, Harry. We did talk about you last night. Alan said he thought you were lying. He said he thought you'd deliberately lied about your friendship with Barbara Smith.

HARRY: (*Angry*) What does he mean – friendship? I never knew the girl. I'd never even seen her until she got into the train at Waterloo.

CAROL stares at him; puzzled, yet obviously impressed.

CAROL: Is that the truth, Harry?

HARRY: Of course it's the truth! Look, Carol – I know certain things have happened – quite extraordinary things, things I can't explain. The theatre ticket; the flowers on the grave; the fact that she was in the same compartment with me on the train … (*Shaking his head*) but I swear to you, I never knew that girl – I'd never seen her in my life before.

CAROL: (*Hesitant*) And you didn't know why she was coming here? You didn't know that …

HARRY: (*Puzzled*) That – what?

CAROL: (*Still hesitating*) That …
HARRY: Go on, Carol.
CAROL: (*Softly; almost frightened to say it*) You didn't
            know that – she was going to kill Mr Fielding?
HARRY: (*Shocked*) Good God, of course I didn't! What a
            thing to say! I hardly knew Tom Fielding. I'd only
            met the man twice, you know that! He was
            practically a stranger to me. (*Taking hold of her
            arm*) Carol, what did Alan Milton really say to you
            last night? (*Tightening his grip*) You've got to tell
            me …

CAROL hesitates: she looks tense, desperately undecided.

CUT TO: The entrance to THOMAS FIELDING Ltd.
*HARRY BRENT's E-type Jaguar is parked near the front gate.
An Austin Mini draws up to the kerb and ALAN gets out. He
looks at the Jaguar for a moment, then turns as HARRY
comes out from the works. He sees ALAN and stops. After a
moment ALAN moves towards HARRY.*

ALAN: Good morning. I didn't expect to find you here.
HARRY: Life's full of surprises.
ALAN: (*Indicates the Jaguar*) Is this yours, Mr Brent?
HARRY: Yes, it is.   (*Indicating the Mini*) Yours, Mr
            Milton?

ALAN smiles.

ALAN: I imagine you've been paying Carol a visit?
HARRY: I'm on my way to Guildford and just dropped in
            for a chat, that's all. Should I have asked your
            permission, Inspector?

ALAN chooses to ignore the remark.

ALAN: I expect Carol told you about Mrs Tolly?
HARRY: Mrs Tolly? Who's Mrs Tolly?
ALAN: They obviously haven't heard the news yet, or
            Carol would have told you. Mrs Tolly used to

work here. She was murdered last night, or rather early this morning. She was found in a flat at Kingsdown Mansions.

HARRY: (*Quietly; after a pause*) How was she murdered?

ALAN: She was strangled.

HARRY: Have you any idea who did it?

ALAN: No, I'm afraid we haven't. Not yet ...

HARRY: Where is Kingsdown Mansions? In Market Weldon?

ALAN: No, Richmond. It's a very nice block of flats facing the river.

ALAN looks at his watch, nods to HARRY. Then crosses towards the entrance to FIELDING's — suddenly he hesitates and turns.

ALAN: Oh, excuse me.

HARRY: (*Also turning*) Yes?

ALAN: When you were down here a week or two ago I believe you borrowed a jacket from Eric Vyner.

HARRY: A jacket?

ALAN: (*Quite friendly*) Yes, you were caught in the rain one afternoon and he lent you an old sports jacket.

HARRY: (*Pleasantly*) Oh, yes, that's right! So he did.

ALAN: What happened to that jacket, Mr Brent?

HARRY: (*Looking at ALAN*) What do you think happened to it? When I borrow things, I return them. (*With a nod*) That's what I did with the jacket.

HARRY opens the door of the Jaguar and gets in.

CUT TO: THOMAS FIELDING's Office.

CAROL is sitting in the armchair listening to ALAN who is questioning her about MRS TOLLY. ALAN is perched on the corner of the desk, facing her.

ALAN: ... Were you surprised when Mrs Tolly gave her notice in?

CAROL: No, I wasn't. I knew she'd been having trouble with her back and she'd been wanting to leave for some time.

ALAN: Carol, I want you to be frank with me about this. Was there anyone here, on the staff, that she was particularly friendly with?

CAROL: No, I don't think so. She was a very efficient person, you know, and most conscientious.

ALAN: That's not what I asked you.

CAROL: Well, I'm afraid I can only tell you what she was like during working hours. She wasn't a friend of mine, so I know very little about her private life. Although one heard rumours, of course.

ALAN: What sort of rumours?

CAROL: Well – you know ...

ALAN: (*Smiling*) No, I don't know. That's what I'm trying to find out.

CAROL: People said that although she and her husband lived together, they – well, they had an arrangement. I don't think there's any doubt that she had boyfriends. She certainly was never short of money.

ALAN rises and moves towards the armchair.

ALAN: Carol, I know you'll probably think this is a ridiculous suggestion, but do you think Tom Fielding was one of her boyfriends?

CAROL: Mr Fielding? Good heavens, no! (*Laughing*) That's absolutely absurd.

ALAN: Why is it absurd? She wasn't a bad looking woman.

CAROL: Yes, but he just wasn't that kind of man.

ALAN: What kind of man was he?

CAROL: Well, he wasn't a "womaniser", I can tell you that.

ALAN: (*Laughing*) I'm not suggesting he was a "womaniser". Good heavens, he was a bachelor; he was entitled to a girl friend or two.

CAROL: Mr Fielding wasn't interested in women; practically his whole life was wrapped up in this business, and when he wasn't here he was either sailing or tinkering with that toy of his.

ALAN: Toy?

CAROL: Well, that's what we used to call it. He was trying to invent a new kind of tape recorder and we used to pull his leg about it, I'm afraid. Years ago, when he was a young man, he invented something to do with a camera – I forget what it was – and sold it to America. Made a great deal of money out of it, at least that's what I've been told. He'd been trying, rather unsuccessfully I'm afraid to do the same thing ever since.

ALAN: Did you ever see the recorder?

CAROL: Yes, he brought it down to the office one day.

ALAN: What happened?

CAROL: It didn't work.

ALAN laughs. The door opens and GEORGE LONGFIELD enters.

GEORGE: Mrs Green's arrived.

CAROL: Yes, all right. I'll be out in a minute.

GEORGE: If you give me the pen, I'll get rid of her for you.

CAROL: Oh, thank you, George.

CAROL crosses to the desk and picks up a fountains pen. She hesitates, then changes her mind.

CAROL: (*To GEORGE*) No, I think perhaps I'd better have a word with her. She's leaving for Canada next week and I probably won't see her again.

GEORGE nods and goes out.

ALAN: Mrs Green's going to Canada?

CAROL: Yes, she's got a daughter out there – she and her husband emigrated about four years ago.

ALAN indicates the pen in CAROL's hand.

ALAN: Well – what's all this about a pen?

CAROL: Apparently Mrs Green gave Mr Fielding this for Christmas and she rang up and asked if she could have it back. (*Faintly amused; shaking her head*) She said it would save her buying a present for her son-in-law. (*She crosses to the door*) Well, it takes all sorts …

ALAN: Carol, wait a minute!

CAROL turns, surprised by ALAN's tone. He moves down to her and takes the fountain pen out of her hand. ALAN looks at the pen.

ALAN: (*After a moment; quietly*) Ask Mrs Green to come in.

CAROL hesitates, as if about to say something, then goes out. ALAN continues examining the pen: suddenly he takes his own fountain pen out of his pocket and compares it with the one in his hand. The two pens are quite different, both in shape and size. He looks towards the door, then – quickly making a decision – puts FIELDING's pen into his pocket instead of his own. He is looking at his own pen when CAROL returns with MRS GREEN. MOLLIE GREEN is a stout, slightly flustered woman, and she is a little embarrassed to find the Inspector in the room.

ALAN: (*Very friendly*) Hello, Mrs Green! Carol – Miss Vyner tells me you're leaving for Canada next week?

MRS GREEN: Yes, I have a married daughter there and – well, Dot's been on to me to join them for some time now. Then when Mr Fielding died … I thought …

82

ALAN: Yes, of course. Well, before you go please leave Miss Vyner your address, just in case we should want to get in touch with you.

MRS GREEN: Yes, I was going to do that anyway.

ALAN smiles at MRS GREEN and hands her his pen.

ALAN: Oh, here's the pen you wanted. The one you gave Mr Fielding.

MRS GREEN: (*Taking pen*) Thank you. (*To CAROL: faintly ill at ease*) I hope you didn't mind about this, Miss Vyner, but I've been put to a lot of expense lately and I thought …

CAROL: No, of course not.

ALAN: (*Pleasantly*) It is the right pen, Mrs Green?

MRS GREEN looks at ALAN then at the pen.

MRS GREEN: Why, yes …

ALAN: (*Laughing*) You should know. You bought it …

MRS GREEN: Yes, of course – of course it's the right one.

ALAN shakes hands with her: for very different reasons they are both pleased with themselves.

ALAN: Goodbye, Mrs Green. I hope you like Canada.

MRS GREEN: Thank you, sir.

CAROL looks at ALAN: she has realised now what has happened.

CAROL: (*To MRS GREEN*) I'll come down with you, Mrs Green.

MRS GREEN: There's no need, my dear.

MRS GREEN goes out followed by CAROL. ALAN takes FIELDING's pen out of his pocket and scrutinises it more closely, trying to unscrew the barrel. After a moment he succeeds, and the pen comes apart in his hands. He moves slowly down to the desk, examining the pen as he does so. CAROL enters. She stands looking at ALAN.

ALAN: (*Looking up*) It seems a perfectly ordinary pen to me. (*He looks down at the pen*) Why the devil did she want this?

CUT TO: A corner table in a self-service café in Market Weldon.

MRS GREEN is sitting at the table drinking a cup of coffee, having just finished lunch. To her surprise ALAN arrives carrying a glass of milk on a tray.

ALAN: Do you mind if I join you?

MRS GREEN: No – no, of course not.

ALAN sits down and disposes of the tray. He starts to sip his milk.

ALAN: What's the fare to Canada, these days? Must be pretty expensive, I should imagine.

MRS GREEN: Oh, it is. It'll cost me the best part of sixty quid by the time I get to Dot's place. She's in Edmonton, you see, right over the other side. And then of course if I don't like it when I get there – but I daren't think about that, I've just got to like it.

ALAN: (*Raising his glass*) Well, I wish you the best of luck, Mrs Green.

MRS GREEN: Thank you.

ALAN: (*Pleasantly*) Oh, before I forget.

He takes FIELDING's pen out of his pocket.

ALAN: I'm afraid I made a mistake. I gave you the wrong pen.

MRS GREEN: The wrong pen?

ALAN: Yes, I'm sorry. I gave you mine, instead of Mr Fielding's.

MRS GREEN looks at ALAN for a moment, then takes his pen out of her handbag. ALAN holds up FIELDING's pen.

84

ALAN: They're not very much alike, are they? I don't know how I came to make such a silly mistake. But then, oddly enough, you didn't spot the difference either.

MRS GREEN looks at him, obviously embarrassed.

ALAN: How much did you pay for this?

MRS GREEN: About – about thirty-five shillings, I think. I can't remember exactly because …

ALAN: (*Quietly*) Because you didn't buy it – did you, Mrs Green?

MRS GREEN: Of course I bought it! I bought it for Mr Fielding's birthday.

ALAN: Really? I thought you bought it him for Christmas. But tell me – where did you buy it from?

MRS GREEN: From – from a shop in the High Street, I just forget the name of the shop, it's – next door to the Post Office.

ALAN: (*Looking at MRS GREEN*) Mrs Green, I'm investigating a murder case – two murders in fact. And if, in my opinion, someone deliberately …

MRS GREEN: Two murders?

ALAN: Yes, a Mrs Tolly was murdered late last night – or rather early this morning. She was strangled.

MRS GREEN: (*Shocked*) Tolly? Phyllis Tolly? The woman who used to work at Fielding's?

ALAN: (*Watching her*) Yes.

MRS GREEN: (*Softly: almost frightened*) Oh, my God …

ALAN: Was she a friend of yours?

MRS GREEN: Yes, she was … Well, no, not exactly a friend, but …

ALAN: Go on, Mrs Green …

85

MRS GREEN: (*Bewildered*) It's – it's her husband that asked me to get ... (*Suddenly*) It's Mr Tolly that wants the pen.

ALAN: (*Quietly surprised*) Mr Tolly?

MRS GREEN: Yes; they both came to see me two or three nights ago. Mrs Tolly and her husband, I mean. She said they were very sorry to hear about Mr Fielding and they wondered if there was anything they could do for me. We sat talking for about half an hour and then just as they were leaving Mr Tolly said he had a customer – he's got a stall in the market, you know ...

ALAN: Yes, I know. Go on.

MRS GREEN: He said he had a customer who was anxious to get hold of something of Mr Fielding's. He said the man was a crank, an absolute nut in fact, but he'd done business with him before and ... Tolly said if I could get that pen he'd give me fifty pounds for it – in cash.

ALAN: Did you ask him why this "customer" of his wanted the pen?

MRS GREEN: Yes; he said he didn't know and he didn't care. It was just a deal so far as he was concerned.

ALAN: (*After a pause*) I hope, for your sake, you're telling me the truth, Mrs Green?

MRS GREEN: I am. Truly, Mr Milton – I really am ... (*She shakes her head; genuinely frightened*) I knew I shouldn't do this ... I knew I was a fool ... But I've had so much expense just lately and what with Mr Fielding ... and ... and ... one thing and another   ...

ALAN: When are you seeing Tolly again?

MRS GREEN: He's supposed to be collecting the pen tonight and handing it over tomorrow morning. It's market day tomorrow.

ALAN hands her FIELDING's pen.

ALAN: Right. Now this is what I want you to do. Don't mention this to anyone. Simply give Tolly the pen and take the fifty pounds. I'll phone you later tonight.

MRS GREEN: (*Perturbed*) Yes, all right, Mr Milton.

ALAN rises, he looks at MRS GREEN, hesitates, then takes pity on her.

ALAN: If you do what I say, you've nothing to worry about.

MRS GREEN nods, but she doesn't look at all happy.

CUT TO: The Clock Square, Market Weldon.

The weekly market is always held in Clock Square and today it is in full swing; the square is occupied with multi-coloured stalls of all shapes and sizes. Crowds of sightseers, hawkers, and local people are milling to and fro between stalls. HAROLD TOLLY – ably assisted by a couple of local boys – occupies one of the largest stalls. They are doing a brisk business in men's ties, pullovers, socks, etc. Nearby a loud-voice character extols the virtues of his "Do-it-yourself" kits. ERIC VYNER can be seen moving from stall to stall, casually interested in the various articles for sale, giving an occasional friendly nod to passing acquaintances.

CUT TO: HAROLD TOLLY's stall in the market. *JACQUELINE DAWSON and MARK RAINER are standing at the stall. MARK is a pleasant, athletic looking man in his early thirties. He wears a double-breasted trench coat and a sports hat. At the moment he is trying to decide whether to buy one of the ties on the stall and JACQUELINE looks thoroughly bored with the proceedings and life in general. HAROLD TOLLY picks up the tie RAINER is interested in and makes an attractive knot with it. RAINER looks at the tie, hesitates, then smiles at HAROLD TOLLY and shakes his head. TOLLY immediately drops the tie and picks up another one.*

TOLLY: They're pure silk, sir. Cut from the square. Guaranteed.

RAINER: (*Dubiously*) Pure silk? (*To JACQUELINE*) Do they look pure silk to you, Jacqueline?

JACQUELINE: They look like hell.

(*RAINER leans forward and feels the tie TOLLY is holding*)

CUT TO: A general view of the market.
ALAN and PHILIPS are standing by a book stall on the fringe of the market. Both men appear to be interested in the lurid display of paperbacks and "True Life" magazines. They wear sports clothes and PHILIPS is smoking a pipe.

PHILIPS: Who's the chap with Jacqueline Dawson?

ALAN: I don't know; I've never seen him before.

MARK RAINER has finally decided not to buy a tie after all, and is shaking his head at a disappointed HAROLD TOLLY.

RAINER: It's not for me. Sorry, old man.

RAINER joins JACQUELINE at the next stall. As he turns away ERIC VYNER passes him. ERIC catches TOLLY's eye, gives a brief nod of recognition, and strolls on.

CUT TO: A Street off the Square.
A taxi draws to a standstill about fifty yards from the Square. KEVIN JASON gets out of the car, pays the driver, and walks towards the market. He is wearing a brand new overcoat and suit and looks distinctly pleased with life.

CUT TO: General View of the market.

ALAN and PHILIPS have left the book stall and are slowly walking through the market towards TOLLY's stall. They have reached the "Do-it-yourself" merchant when ALAN suddenly takes hold of his companion's arm.

ALAN: Roy, there's the man I told you about! … The one
          who was in my flat … The chap who wanted the
          cigarettes.

KEVIN JASON is strolling through the market when he suddenly sees ALAN staring at him. He stops dead in his tracks. For a brief moment the two men stand looking at each other, then JASON quickly turns and makes for an opening between two nearby stalls. ALAN and PHILIPS set off in pursuit of him. JASON is now trying desperately hard to find a new way out of the market place for, unfortunately for him, a barrow boy (complete with a well-stocked fruit barrow) has suddenly appeared in the opening between the two stalls. ALAN has almost caught up with JASON; suddenly the Irishman makes a decision and with a quick turn charges headlong into the barrow boy. The boy is knocked off balance – the barrow topples over, crashing into a stall. In a matter of seconds JASON has leapt over the barrow and is disappearing between the stalls. A bad-tempered ALAN and an irate PHILIPS are trying to fight their way through a mass of people and a sea of fruit. By now the barrow boy is pursuing a violent argument with the owner of the stall.

CUT TO: A Street near the Square.

KEVIN JASON is running away from the market, heading for the High Street. In the background, ALAN and PHILIPS have finally extricated themselves and are in pursuit of the Irishman.

CUT TO: A Street Corner in Market Weldon.

Two uniformed policemen – BOOTH and SANDERSON – are sitting in a police car on the corner of the High Street. Suddenly, through the windscreen of the Zephyr, we see KEVIN JASON. He is running like mad; ALAN and PHILIPS are in pursuit, having obviously gained ground. BOOTH recognises ALAN MILTON and immediately jumps out of the car and races across the road in an attempt to "head off" JASON. BOOTH finally catches up with JASON and with a flying tackle brings the Irishman to the ground. JASON is struggling, making a last desperate attempt to free himself.

CUT TO: ALAN MILTON's Office.

PHILIPS is sitting at a desk writing a report on the morning's events. ALAN enters; he carries a manilla folder and a notebook. PHILIPS rises.

ALAN: I've spent half an hour with our Irish friend. He won't tell me a damn thing. Not even his name. (*Indicating a collection of articles on the desk*) Have you been through his things?

PHILIPS: Yes, there's nothing there I'm afraid, and so far the Yard haven't come up with anything.

ALAN: (*Irritated*) Who the devil is this character, Roy?

PHILIPS: Search me.

ALAN: Anyway, I'm charging him. He broke into my flat and he was carrying a gun, that's enough for me.

PHILIPS: I've had an interesting talk with Mr Tolly. Do you know what his story is? He says he knows nothing whatever about the pen, he's never seen our Irish chum in his life before, and he claims that six months ago he borrowed fifty quid from Mrs Green and last night …

ALAN: And last night repaid it! Oh, my God – that's a likely story!

PHILIPS: It's a very good story so far as he's concerned.
There is a knock on the door and PC BOOTH enters.
BOOTH: Excuse me, Inspector.
ALAN: Come in, Booth! Are you feeling all right now?
BOOTH: Yes, I'm fine, sir. Thank you. (*Smiling*) Quite enjoyed this morning, Inspector – in a curious sort of way.
ALAN: Yes, well – in a curious sort of way I didn't.
BOOTH: (*Handing ALAN a driving licence*) Someone's just handed in this driving licence, sir – they found it in the market. I think our friend might have dropped it.
ALAN examines the driving licence.
ALAN: Kevin Jason … Kingsdown Mansions, Richmond …
ALAN glances at PHILIPS
PHILIPS: (*Surprised*) Kingsdown Mansions?
ALAN: (*Pleased*) Thank you, Booth.
ALAN crosses towards the hat stand, followed by PHILIPS.

CUT TO: The Entrance Hall of Kingsdown Mansions.
REG BRYER is standing near the lift talking to ALAN and SERGEANT PHILIPS. He wears a dark blue double-breasted suit, and a regimental tie.
REG: … Good heavens, of course I know Jason! Thick-set chap; Irish accent; natty dresser … Been here about six months, I should think … He's on the top floor, number 56 …
ALAN: What does Mr Jason do, exactly?
REG: Do? Haven't a clue. Calls himself a business consultant, but that could mean any damn thing. Tried to consult him myself once; little matter of a fiver. Didn't get very far.

PHILIPS: All right, Mr Bryer, take us upstairs. We want to see his flat.

REG: What if he's in?

ALAN: He's not in. But I've got a warrant, if that's worrying you, Mr Bryer.

REG looks at ALAN then turns towards the lift.

CUT TO: The Drawing Room of KEVIN JASON's Flat, Kingsdown Mansions.

In shape and size this is very similar to the main room of Flat 18. But here the similarity ends; MR JASON has furnished his home with considerable thought and care. He is fastidious about his surroundings as well as his clothes. REG BRYER enters from the hall followed by ALAN and PHILIPS. REG has a bunch of keys in his hand.

REG: It's pretty much the same as the other flat. Miss Stafford's – or Tolly – or whatever her name was. (*Pointing to doors*) There's the main bedroom, guest-room, kitchen, bathrooms ... There's a storeroom through there, not very large.

ALAN: (*Dismissing him*) Thank you. That's all right, Mr Bryer.

REG: If there's anything I can do, Inspector ...

ALAN: We'll let you know.

REG: Oh – there's just one thing. Supposing Mr Jason shows up while you're here?

ALAN: He won't.

REG: Oh. (*Looks at PHILIPS*) Oh, I see.

He goes out into the hall and after a moment we hear the front door close.

ALAN: (*To PHILIPS*) Go through this room, I'll take a quick look round.

PHILIPS: Right.

PHILIPS crosses to a writing bureau and starts to examine the drawers. ALAN goes into the guest-room.

CUT TO: The Guest-Room of KEVIN JASON's Flat.

This is a medium sized room and was of course intended as an extra bedroom. JASON, a cine enthusiast, has converted it into a projection room. There is a large table near the door with a telephone on it, scribbling pad, a spool of film and a 16mm movie projector. At the far end of the room a screen suspends from the ceiling blocking out the light from the window.

ALAN has switched on the light and is looking at the equipment with interest; a film has been threaded into the projector and is obviously ready for showing. ALAN moves slowly round the table, looking at the projector.

ALAN: (*Calling*) Roy!

ALAN is examining the film when PHILIPS enters. After a moment he looks up.

ALAN: You go in for this sort of thing, don't you?

PHILIPS moves to the table, obviously intrigued with the projector

PHILIPS: Yes, but my projector isn't as good as this – unfortunately.

ALAN: Can you work this one?

PHILIPS: (*Amused*) Why, yes, I think so.

ALAN: (*Seriously*) Go ahead. I want to take a look at this film.

PHILIPS looks at ALAN, arrested by his tone of voice, then he turns towards the table again. He studies the projector for a moment then gives a reassuring nod.

PHILIPS: Switch the light out.

ALAN switches out the light as PHILIPS starts to run the film. The two men watch the screen. They see various shots of the River Thames – a quiet, secluded part of the river. The camera very slowly pans to show a cabin cruiser anchored near the bank. The name of the cabin cruiser, "Horizon" is clearly visible. A tall, heavily built man stands with his back to the camera untying a rope. He wears sports clothes, an old yachting cap, and has an empty pipe in his mouth. After a moment the man turns, and we see then that it is TOM FIELDING. He is obviously unaware of being filmed. PHILIPS looks at ALAN.

PHILIPS: That's Tom Fielding.

ALAN nods, his eyes still on the film. On the screen TOM FIELDING has turned towards the hatch and is calling down the companionway to someone in the cabin below.

ALAN: There's someone else on that boat …

On the screen we see that FIELDING has now turned away from the hatch and is busy filling his pipe from a tobacco pouch. He looks happy and contented. After a little while a man comes slowly up the companionway and stands looking across at FIELDING, smiling at him. It is HARRY BRENT.

END OF EPISODE THREE

EPISODE FOUR

THE PROBLEM

OPEN TO: The Guest Room of KEVIN JASON's Flat.

The film is being projected onto the screen at the far end of the room. On the screen TOM FIELDING has turned towards the hatch and is calling down the companionway to someone in the cabin below.

ALAN's VOICE: There's someone else on that boat …

On the screen we see that FIELDING has now turned away from the hatch and is busy filling his pipe from a tobacco pouch. He looks happy and contented. After a little while HARRY BRENT comes slowly up the companionway and stands looking across at FIELDING, smiling at him. FIELDING turns and joins HARRY at the hatch; the two men stand talking, they are obviously good friends. The film flickers to a finish. As the film finishes PHILIPS stops the projector and looks across at ALAN.

PHILIPS: When do you think this was taken?

ALAN: It's difficult to say, but judging from the weather and the foliage I should imagine about two months ago.

PHILIPS: Yes, that's my bet. (*Indicating the projector*) Well, this proves one thing. Mrs Tolly could have been telling the truth about the coffee bar meeting. Harry Brent obviously knew Fielding – knew him before Carol introduced them in the Falstaff that night.

ALAN: Yes. (*Irritated and puzzled*) But why the devil didn't Harry tell Carol he was a friend of Fielding's?

PHILIPS: Why didn't Tom Fielding tell her?

ALAN: (*Nodding*) That's a good question, Roy.

PHILIPS picks up the film on the table.

PHILIPS: Shall we run this one through as well?

ALAN: Yes, let's take a look at it.

PHILIPS turns towards the projector and as he does so the telephone rings. ALAN looks at PHILIPS. The phone continues ringing. ALAN hesitates, then picks up the receiver.

ALAN: (*On phone*) Hello?

OPERATOR: (*On the other end*) Richmond 7942?

ALAN: (*Quickly looking at the dial*) Speaking …

OPERATOR: This is Telegrams. I have a telegram for a Mr Kevin Jason, 56 Kingsdown Mansions, Richmond.

ALAN: Thank you. I'll take it down.

He takes a pen from his pocket. PHILIPS takes an envelope from his pocket and hands it to ALAN.

OPERATOR: (*Reading*) Brent arrives Positano eight o'clock tonight …

ALAN: (*Writing*) Brent arrives Positano eight o'clock tonight … And the name of the sender?

OPERATOR: I'm sorry, there isn't a signature. Do you wish me to confirm this telegram?

ALAN: (*Hesitating*) Er – yes. Yes, please do that.

OPERATOR: (*Ringing off*) Thank you.

PHILIPS looks at the envelope.

PHILIPS: Does that mean Harry Brent?

ALAN: (*After a moment*) What's your guess, Roy?

CUT TO: CAROL VYNER's Office at THOMAS FIELDING Ltd.

CAROL has now moved into a small secretarial office. She is sitting at a desk typing a letter. There is a knock on the door and ERIC pops his head into the office.

ERIC: May I come in?

CAROL rises: she is obviously surprised to see her brother.

CAROL: Hello, Eric! What are you doing here?

ERIC: Can you spare a minute?

CAROL:	Yes, of course. (*Puzzled*) Is anything the matter?
ERIC:	I think you said you were seeing Harry tonight?
CAROL:	Yes, I am. I told you – we're having dinner together in Town.
ERIC:	Well – ask him to phone me, Carol. Any time tonight, I'll be in all evening.
CAROL:	Can't I deliver a message?
ERIC:	(*Shaking his head*) I think perhaps I'd better have a word with him myself, Carol. I tried to get him on the phone this morning but …
CAROL:	Eric, what is it? You're being very mysterious.
ERIC:	A young chap named Robson came to see me this morning – Sergeant Robson. I think he's one of Alan's men. Anyway, he's with the C.I.D.
CAROL:	Well?
ERIC:	He questioned me about the jacket, the one I lent Harry.
CAROL:	Why on earth are they interested in that wretched jacket? I should have thought …
ERIC:	They've a very good reason for being interested in it. It was found at Richmond – in Mrs Tolly's flat.
CAROL:	<u>Your</u> jacket?
ERIC:	Yes. When Alan spoke to me about the jacket I told him the truth. I said I'd lent it to Harry and he hadn't returned it. Unfortunately, Harry didn't confirm my story.
CAROL:	What do you mean?
ERIC:	He told Alan that he had returned the jacket to me.

CAROL: (*Puzzled*) Why should he say that?

ERIC: I don't know why …

CAROL: But surely he must know whether … (*Suddenly*) Leave it with me, Eric. I'll have a word with Harry about it tonight.

ERIC: (*Turning towards the door*) Yes, all right, Carol.

CAROL: I shouldn't worry about it, Eric.

ERIC: Well, I am worried. You know me. I like to get things cut and dried. Besides, I … (*Hesitates*)

CAROL: Go on …

ERIC: I was going to say I knew Mrs Tolly. I'd spoken to her. We weren't friends, of course, but – well, I don't suppose Harry had even heard of the woman before she was murdered.

CAROL: (*Quietly*) I'm sure there's a perfectly simple explanation for all this.

ERIC: What train are you coming back on?

CAROL: It'll be the last one – the eleven-thirty, I imagine. But don't bother to meet me. I can pick up a cab.

ERIC: I'll be there. I'll be in the car park.

(*He opens the door*)

CAROL: There's no need, Eric.

CUT TO: ALAN MILTON's Office.

ALAN is sitting at his desk questioning HAROLD TOLLY who sits opposite him. TOLLY wears a check sports jacket and the usual buttonhole; he looks distinctly agitated and annoyed.

TOLLY: … Look, I've told you. I don't know this fellow Jason, I've never seen him before!

ALAN: He was on his way to your stall, Mr Tolly, when he spotted me and made a dash for it.

TOLLY: How do you know that? He might have been meeting someone – he might have been going to one of the other stalls for all you know!

ALAN: We think he was going to your stall, Mr Tolly.

TOLLY: Well, he wasn't. I tell you I don't know this man. Never seen him before – never ever heard of him!

ALAN: All right, let's leave Mr Jason for the moment and talk about Mrs Green.

TOLLY: (*Truculently*) What about Mrs Green?

ALAN: You gave her fifty pounds.

TOLLY: That's right. She lent me fifty quid some time back. I repaid her.

ALAN: That's not what Mrs Green says. She says you asked her to get a pen for you – Tom Fielding's pen. She says that's why you paid her the fifty pounds.

TOLLY: Are you kidding? Fifty quid for a pen? Do you think I'm nuts?

ALAN: (*Irritated; rising*) No, I don't think you're nuts, Mr Tolly. But I don't think you're telling the truth either. Kevin Jason asked you to get that pen for him and it's my bet he offered you a great deal more than fifty pounds for it!

TOLLY: (*Annoyed*) I've told you, I don't know this chap Jason! I've never seen him before! Look – if you're not going to believe a word I say, what's the point of asking me questions?

ALAN: Mr Tolly, you're a businessman – you have a great many "contacts", a great many "friends".

TOLLY: Well?

ALAN: Yet you expect me to believe that when you needed money you went straight to Mrs Green?

ALAN shakes his head and presses the button on the desk. TOLLY rises.

TOLLY: I tried other people first. I tried a hell of a lot of people, but they just wouldn't play.

ALAN: No, and I'm not playing either. Go away, Tolly – think things over. When you're prepared to tell the truth give me a ring.

TOLLY: I've told you the truth!

The door opens and TOMLINS enters.

ALAN: Mr Tolly's leaving.

TOMLINS: Yes, sir. (*To TOLLY*) Sergeant Croft would like a word with you, sir.

TOLLY: (*Still smarting from ALAN's remarks*) Who the hell is Sergeant Croft?

ALAN: (*Returning to his desk*) I've asked him to take your fingerprints. That is – if you've no objections?

TOLLY: And supposing I do object?

ALAN: (*Pleasantly*) Then we don't take them, Mr Tolly.

TOLLY: Why – why do you want my fingerprints anyway?

ALAN: (*A shrug*) It's just routine.

TOLLY: I don't believe that. You must have a reason.

ALAN: (*Looking at TOLLY*) Yes, we have a reason. We found a number of fingerprints in your wife's flat at Richmond. We'd like to compare them with yours.

TOLLY: But – I've never been to that flat. I knew nothing about it.

ALAN: Then you've nothing to worry about, have you, Mr Tolly?

TOLLY hesitates, looks at ALAN, then goes out with TOMLINS. ALAN picks up the phone.

ALAN: (*On phone*) Get me Miss Carol Vyner at Thomas Fielding's …

He replaces the receiver and picks up a letter from the desk. He is reading the letter when the door opens, and PHILIPS appears in the doorway. He is wearing his outdoor clothes.

PHILIPS: I'm just leaving. Give me twenty minutes and I'll be ready for you.

ALAN: Right! Thank you, Roy.

The phone rings. ALAN reaches for the receiver.

CUT TO: CAROL's Office at THOMAS FIELDING Ltd. *Carol has just finished typing a letter and is removing the notepaper from the machine when the phone rings. She picks up the receiver. For the rest of this conversation, we cut back and forth between CAROL and ALAN.*

CAROL: (*On phone*) Carol Vyner speaking …

ALAN: (*On phone*) Carol – this is Alan …

CAROL: Oh, hello, Alan!

ALAN: Carol, I've got to see you. I'll pick you up in about fifteen minutes.

CAROL: I'm sorry, Alan, I'm terribly busy and I'm going up to Town this evening. If you could leave it over until tomorrow …

ALAN: (*Curtly*) Meet me outside Fielding's; I'm leaving straight away.

CAROL: (*Annoyed*) I'm sorry, it's impossible. I'm up to my neck in work!

ALAN: This is important, Carol.

CAROL: It may be important to you, Alan!

ALAN: It's important to you too. It's about Harry. I'll pick you up in exactly fifteen minutes.

ALAN rings off. CAROL still holds the phone; she looks annoyed, yet curious. She slowly replaces the receiver.

CUT TO: The Main Entrance to Thomas Fielding Ltd. *ALAN drives up in his car just as CAROL emerges from the office block. She crosses towards the Mini as ALAN climbs out of the car and opens the passenger door.*

103

CAROL: (*Irritated*) Alan, what's this all about? We're terribly busy this afternoon.

ALAN: Jump in, Carol. I'll have you back here by half past four, I promise you.

CAROL: (*Still hesitant*) But where are we going? I can't just run away from the office without …

ALAN: For God's sake stop arguing and get in the car!

CAROL: I refuse to get in this car until you tell me where we're going!

ALAN: (*With sarcasm*) I'm not trying to abduct you, Carol. You'll be quite safe, I assure you. Now get in the car.

CAROL gives him a "look", hesitates, then gets into the car.

CUT TO: A county lane, Market Weldon.

ALAN's car draws to a standstill outside a small house in a country lane. ALAN gets out of the car followed by Carol. She looks at the house, then at ALAN – obviously still puzzled. ALAN takes CAROL by the arm and leads her towards the house. As they approach the house PHILIPS come out of the front door and gives a friendly wave. He is obviously expecting them.

CUT TO: A Bedroom in ROY PHILIPS' house.

The room has been "converted" into a projection room for ROY PHILIPS, who is obviously a home movie enthusiast. *CAROL enters the room followed by ALAN and PHILIPS. PHILIPS smiles at CAROL and indicates the only comfortable chair in the room.*

PHILIPS: Do sit down, Miss Vyner …

PHILIPS crosses to the projector which is on a small table near the wall. CAROL stares at the equipment in amazement; she is more bewildered than ever.

ALAN: Carol, we're going to show you two pictures – two short films. Now let me explain about these films. An Irishman called Kevin Jason was arrested this morning. He broke into my flat a few days ago and we're holding him on a housebreaking charge. Jason has a flat in Kingsdown Mansions, Richmond, and …

CAROL: Kingsdown Mansions? Isn't that where Mrs Tolly was found?

ALAN: Yes, it is. We searched Jason's flat and we found two films. Fortunately, Roy here is an expert on that sort of thing …

PHILIPS: An amateur, Inspector – not an expert!

ALAN: Anyway, we took a look at them. The first film – which we'll show you in a few minutes – proves without any shadow of doubt that Harry Brent was a friend – a very good friend, I would say – of Tom Fielding's. But the second film we saw is the one that we're really interested in, and this is the one we're going to show you first. Okay, Roy?

PHILIPS: Yes, I'm ready.

CAROL: Wait a minute! Did this man, Jason – did he take these films?

ALAN: I should imagine so, but we don't know – not for certain. They were obviously taken without the people concerned – the people in the film, I mean – realising it.

PHILIPS: I should imagine this one was taken from inside a van – or from the back of a parked car, perhaps.

ALAN: (*Nods*) Go ahead, Roy …

PHILIPS turns off the light and switches on the projector. CAROL, puzzled, yet obviously intrigued by the turn of events, sits in the armchair. ALAN perches himself on the arm. They watch the screen at the far end of the room. We see a side street in KENSINGTON, London; the camera concentrating on the entrance to a double-fronted shop – a travel bureau bearing the name "HARRY BRENT Ltd." A taxi draws up in front of the shop and JACQUELINE DAWSON gets out of it followed by TOM FIELDING ...

CAROL: That's Jacqueline Dawson ... and Mr Fielding.

ALAN: Yes, that's right.

On the screen TOM FIELDING pays the taxi driver, then turning takes hold of JACQUELINE's arm and escorts her into the shop. The film flickers, as if it is about to finish.

ALAN: (*Turning to CAROL*) Now these next shots were obviously taken on a different day. Try and remember when it was, Carol.

CAROL looks at him puzzled. ALAN points to the screen. On the screen the film flickers into life again. We see the same street; the entrance to "HARRY BRENT Ltd." The weather has changed slightly; there are different cars parked in the street, different travel posters in the shop window. A sports car appears from the right and stops in front of the shop. The driver – MARK RAINER – gets out of the car and crosses toward "HARRY BRENT Ltd". RAINER still wears the trench-style coat and sports hat. As he reaches the window CAROL comes out of the shop. She sees RAINER and immediately recognises him. They stand chatting, CAROL obviously amused by something RAINER is telling her. After a moment RAINER raises his hat and goes into the shop. CAROL crosses to the kerb; she stares up and down the street, looking for a taxi. The film gradually flickers to a finish. PHILIPS turns on the light and stops the projector. He starts to change the film. ALAN has risen and is looking down at CAROL.

ALAN: Do you remember when that was taken?

106

CAROL: (*Bewildered*) Why, yes. It – it was about three weeks ago. Three weeks last Saturday, I think. But why should anyone photograph me?

ALAN: (*Ignoring the question*) Who was the man – the man you were talking to?

CAROL: His name's Rainer – Mark Rainer. He's a friend of Harry's.

PHILIPS: And Jacqueline Dawson's.

CAROL: Jacqueline Dawson?

PHILIPS: Yes, they were in the market together. We saw them this morning – just before we picked up Jason.

CAROL: Is this true, Alan?

ALAN: Yes, it is. Tell us all you know about Mr Rainer.

CAROL: He's a friend of Harry's; quite an old friend, I should imagine. We all had dinner together about four or five weeks ago, that was the first time I met him.

ALAN: What does he do?

CAROL: I think he's with Thomas Cook's or American Express, or someone like that. He's a very pleasant man – appears to be interested in cars more than anything else. That's about all I can tell you about him.

ALAN: Is he married?

CAROL: No, I don't … No, I'm sure he isn't.

ALAN: Does he live in Town?

CAROL: I honestly don't know.

ALAN: Thank you, Carol.

PHILIPS: (*To ALAN*) I'm ready.

ALAN: Carol, did Tom Fielding have a boat – a cabin cruiser – called "Horizon"?

CAROL: Yes, he did. He used to keep it at Marlow and go down for weekends. But he sold it.

ALAN: When?

CAROL: Oh – some time ago. Must be getting on for a year
          now.

ALAN looks at PHILIPS.

ALAN: Carol, what would you say if I told you – he once
          invited your fiancé down to Marlow?

CAROL: Harry? But he couldn't have done! He didn't know
          Harry until I introduced …

She stares at ALAN, then looks across at the projector.

ALAN: (*To PHILIPS; quietly*) Go ahead, Roy …

PHILIPS switches on the projector.

CUT TO: The entrance to THOMAS FIELDING Ltd.
*ALAN's mini draws to a standstill about thirty yards or so
from the entrance.*

CUT TO: Inside the car.

*ALAN is sitting at the wheel, next to CAROL who looks both
worried and introspective. He looks at her for a moment
without speaking, and glances at his watch.*

ALAN: I said I'd get you back by half-past four. It's five
          and twenty past.

CAROL: Thank you.

ALAN: You look worried, Carol.

CAROL: Is it surprising? (*Looking at ALAN*) You've finally
          succeeded, Alan.

ALAN: Succeeded?

CAROL: You've convinced me that the man I'm going to
          marry is a liar. You've proved to me that …

ALAN: (*Interrupting her; curtly*) Now wait a minute! That
          wasn't the object of the exercise. I'm not
          interested in Harry Brent because he's your fiancé!
          I'm interested in him because, in some curious
          way, he's mixed up in the Fielding murder.

CAROL: You think he knew that Tom Fielding was going to be murdered?

ALAN: I think he knew that it was on the cards – yes. (*Suddenly*) Carol, there's something I want to ask you. Now be honest with me, please. The other night I told you about Barbara Smith; I told you what she said just before she died.

CAROL: Well?

ALAN: Did you repeat what I told you – to Harry, I mean?

CAROL: No, I didn't. But … (*Hesitant*) … he knew we'd been discussing him. He sensed it in the car when we were going to the station. The next morning, he turned up at the office. He said he was worried; that he knew we'd been talking about him the night before.

ALAN: Go on …

CAROL: It was a difficult situation, Alan. I had to tell him something … I told him you didn't believe his story about the girl. I told him you felt sure that he'd met her before somewhere. (*Shaking her head*) But I didn't tell him what she'd said; that she'd actually mentioned his name … I didn't, truly, Alan …

ALAN looks at her for a moment.

ALAN: Carol, what do you really know about Harry Brent?

CAROL shrugs

ALAN: You met him by accident, he told you he came from Market Weldon, he invited you out to dinner, and then – hey presto! – you were engaged.

CAROL: I fell in love with him. When you're in love with someone you trust them.

ALAN: Do you still trust him, Carol?

CAROL: I – I don't know.

CAROL turns to open the door and ALAN stops her, his hand on her arm.

ALAN: Carol, wait a minute. When are you seeing Harry again?

CAROL: Tonight. We're having dinner together.

ALAN: (*Surprised*) In Town?

CAROL: Yes.

ALAN: (*Casually*) I thought he was abroad, in Italy or somewhere …?

CAROL: No. (*Puzzled*) What made you think that?

ALAN: (*Shrugs; dismissing the matter*) I don't know. Just something you said, I suppose. (*Squeezing CAROL's arm*) If anything happens, Carol – if you get worried about anything, it doesn't matter how trivial if might seem – you know where I am, darling.

CAROL looks at ALAN for a moment, then with a little nod releases her arm and opens the car door.

CAROL: Thank you, Alan …

CUT TO: Fulton Street, Bloomsbury. Night.

A taxi turns off the main road into this quiet street and pulls up in front of a small restaurant. There are one or two shops in the street and several houses; an old-fashioned block of flats, Fulton Court, faces the shops. CAROL gets out of the taxi, pays the driver, and hurries into the restaurant. As CAROL goes through the door into the entrance hall of the establishment, we see an ornate sign over the door that reads "Positano Restaurant".

CUT TO: A corner of the Positano Restaurant.

HARRY is sitting at a table drinking a dry martini and patiently waiting for CAROL. She suddenly appears followed by a WAITER, who is taking her coat from her as she approaches the table. HARRY rises.

CAROL: Harry, I'm terribly sorry – the train was fifteen minutes late and when I arrived at the station, I simply couldn't get a taxi ...

HARRY: (*Amused*) Don't worry, Carol. (*Kissing her*) I was late anyway ...

CAROL: I should have come up by car, Eric wanted me to.

CAROL is obviously a little nervous, faintly ill at ease. HARRY is quick to notice this. He holds the chair for CAROL as she sits at the table. HARRY returns to his place.

HARRY: How is Eric?

CAROL: He's fine, he sends his love. (*She arranges herself; putting her handbag on the table*) Well, I say he's fine – he's not really, he's a little worried at the moment.

HARRY: (*Looking at CAROL*) Oh? What's he worried about? (*To WAITER*) Two dry martinis.

WAITER: Yes, sir.

CAROL: (*Looking at HARRY*) The police have been to see him; twice, as a matter of fact. They keep on asking him questions about that jacket.

HARRY: Which jacket?

CAROL: The sports jacket – the one you borrowed from him. You remember, you got wet one afternoon and borrowed a jacket.

HARRY: Yes, of course I remember! You know, this is very odd. Your ex-boyfriend, Alan Milton, questioned me about ...

CAROL: (*Irritated*) I do wish you wouldn't keep calling Alan my ex-boyfriend!

HARRY: Oh, I'm sorry, darling. (*Smiling at her*) You're very touchy, Carol. Are you sure it's Eric that's worried, and not you?

111

CAROL: Well, naturally, if Eric's worried, I'm worried.

HARRY: Yes, but what exactly is he worried about? He lent me the jacket and I returned it.

CAROL: But that's just the point. Eric says you didn't return it.

HARRY: He says I didn't return it?

CAROL: Yes.

HARRY: (*Unconcerned*) Well, I thought I did. I was pretty sure I ... (*He smiles at CAROL again*) ... Maybe I didn't. (*A shrug*) Perhaps I've still got the coat. Tell Eric I'll take another look.

CAROL: Harry, I don't think you understand! The police have got the jacket. It was found in a flat at Richmond – the flat where Mrs Tolly was murdered. Naturally, the police want to know how it got there.

HARRY: Well, I didn't take it there. I didn't even know Mrs Tolly.

CAROL: (*Slowly; looking at him*) No, but Eric did ...

HARRY: Good Lord, you're not trying to tell me the police suspect dear old Eric?

CAROL: (*"On edge"*) I don't know whether they suspect him or not, but they want to know how his jacket got into Mrs Tolly's flat! And frankly, I don't blame them.

HARRY: Neither do I. But, obviously, they're barking up the wrong tree. I didn't take it there, and I shouldn't imagine Eric did.

CAROL: No, of course he didn't. (*Puzzled*) Harry, are you sure – quite sure – that you returned it?

HARRY: No, I've told you, I'm not sure – not a hundred per cent. I thought I did. (*Patting her hand*) Stop worrying, Carol! Look, I'll have a word with your ex ... with Milton about this. I'll tell him that I'm not absolutely sure that I did return the jacket after all. How's that?

CAROL: Then they'll start questioning you.

HARRY: That's fine! That's okay by me. So long as you stop worrying!

CAROL looks at him; she is still on edge, mystified by his manner, yet grateful for the suggestion he has made. The WAITER arrives with the drinks.

WAITER: It was two dry martinis, sir?

HARRY: It was – it was indeed.

He gives CAROL a reassuring smile.

CUT TO: Fulton Street, Bloomsbury.

A MOTOR CYCLIST drives down the street, finally stopping at the block of flats opposite the restaurant. The man – BRIAN FILEY – gets off the bike and starts to unstrap a violin case which has been carefully fastened to the pillion. FILEY is about the same age as HARRY BRENT; a ruthless, calculating man whom, curiously enough, women find irresistible. He takes the violin case and goes into Fulton Court, the block of flats.

CUT TO: The front door of Flat 19A, a third floor flat in Fulton Court.

FILEY is standing at the door, finger on the bell button. The door is opened by REG BRYER. He is wearing grey flannel trousers and a blazer; he carries a pair of binoculars in his hand. BRYER gives FILEY a brief nod and beckons him into the flat.

CUT TO: The Living room of 19A Fulton Court.

This is a large, cheaply furnished room, with a bay window over-looking the Positano Restaurant. A settee has been drawn up to the window. REG enters followed by FILEY.

REG: I thought you were never coming.

FILEY ignores REG, and crossing the room puts the violin case down on a table near the settee.

FILEY: Have they arrived?

REG: Yes, Brent arrived about ten past nine. The girl was very late.

FILEY nods, opens the violin case, and takes out a Waldofleischer automatic rifle; it is fitted with a telescopic sight. FILEY examines the sight. REG stands watching him.

FILEY: (*Looking at REG*) I was expecting Jason to be here. Why you, Bryer?

REG: Jason couldn't make it.

FILEY: Why not?

REG: The police picked him up; they're still holding him.

FILEY is still interested in the rifle, but his voice betrays a degree of anxiety.

FILEY: When did this happen?

REG: This morning – in Market Weldon.

FILEY: The bloody fool.

REG: We all make mistakes, Filey.

FILEY: Not in this game, Bryer. Just one. That's all – just one …

FILEY crosses to the settee with the rifle. He stands looking out of the window. After a moment he raises the rifle and focuses it on the restaurant. We see the sign "Positano Restaurant" through the telescopic sight of the rifle. FILEY slowly lowers the rifle and sits on the arm of the settee.

REG: Will it be difficult?

FILEY: Shouldn't think so.

FILEY puts the rifle down on the table and takes a packet of cigarettes out of his pocket and a lighter.

FILEY: I take it it's just Brent he wants?

REG: No, Brent and the girl.

FILEY: (*Very surprised*) And the girl? Are you sure?

REG: Of course I'm sure!

FILEY: (*Puzzled*) That's what he said – Brent <u>and</u> the girl.

REG: (*Tensely: "on edge"*) That's what he said, Filey! Take Brent first, in case there's a slip up.

FILEY looks at REG, obviously still puzzled, then he nods and flicks his lighter.

CUT TO: A corner of the Positano Restaurant. As before. *HARRY is lighting a cigarette. He and CAROL have now reached the coffee stage. CAROL still looks worried and faintly ill at ease.*

HARRY: Are you sure you wouldn't like a liqueur?

CAROL: Yes, I'm quite sure.

HARRY: Have a brandy.

CAROL: No, thank you, Harry.

HARRY: What time's your train?

CAROL: Eleven-thirty.

HARRY: (*Looking at his watch*) You've plenty of time. It'll only take ten minutes to the station.

CAROL: (*Nods; then pauses. Making conversation*) Where's your car, I didn't notice it?

HARRY: It's just round the corner.

CAROL: Oh …

HARRY: (*Watching her*) In Blandford Street.

CAROL: Oh, I see. (*A moment*) Well – thank you, Harry.

HARRY: For what?

CAROL: For dinner.

HARRY: (*With a suggestion of a smile*) For one horrible moment I thought you were going to say, "For a very pleasant evening." That's the usual phrase, surely. Except that it hasn't been a very pleasant evening, has it, Carol?

CAROL looks at HARRY and waits a moment.

115

CAROL: (*Tensely*) Why dd you lie to me, Harry? Why on earth didn't you tell me that Mr Fielding was a friend of yours?

HARRY: He wasn't a friend of mine. I only met him twice. The first time was when …

CAROL: Don't lie, Harry! (*Shaking her head*) Please, don't lie! I know you were a friend of his. I just don't understand why you didn't tell me about it. That night – in the Falstaff – I introduced you to each other. You both acted as if you were strangers, as if you'd never met before … Why? Why, Harry?

HARRY: (*Quietly, after a moment*) Who told you I was a friend of Tom's? Mrs Tolly?

CAROL: Mrs Tolly?

HARRY: Yes, she saw us one night in a coffee bar. It was a hundred to one chance, but unfortunately … (*He stops, looks at CAROL*) Was it Mrs Tolly?

CAROL: No …

HARRY: Then who told you?

CAROL: I saw some photographs – pictures …

HARRY: (*Curious*) Pictures? Of me, and Tom Fielding?

CAROL: Yes; someone took some cine pictures of you and … Harry, why didn't you and Mr Fielding tell me that you knew each other?

HARRY: Wait a minute! (*Quietly; yet with a sudden authority*) Carol, tell me about these pictures. Where did you see them?

CAROL: (*Hesitant*) A friend of mine showed them to me.

HARRY: When?

CAROL: This – this afternoon.

HARRY: Was it the Inspector?

CAROL doesn't reply.

HARRY: It must have been Milton! (*Quickly, taking hold of her hand, before she can withdraw it*) Carol, this is

116

important! Tell me about these pictures. What did you see?

CAROL looks at HARRY, surprised by the sudden change in his manner.

CAROL: You were on a boat – Mr Fielding's boat – on the river somewhere. (*She hesitates and HARRY slowly releases her hand*) You were talking to each other. You were obviously very good friends …

HARRY: Go on …

CAROL: There were other pictures too, taken outside of your office … Mr Fielding getting out of a cab with Jacqueline Dawson … Me … talking to Mark Rainer …

HARRY: Where did Milton get these films – who gave them to him?

CAROL: I – I don't know.

HARRY: (*Tensely*) You must know, Carol!

CAROL: (*Shaking her head, determined not to tell him*) I don't know where he got them from …

There is a pause; HARRY is deep in thought. Suddenly he makes a decision and rises from the table.

HARRY: (*To passing WAITER*) Bring me my bill, please – straight away. (*To CAROL*) Get your coat, we're leaving!

CAROL stares at him, too astonished to be annoyed.

CUT TO: The living room of Flat 19A, Fulton Court. As before.

REG BRYER is standing by the window watching the restaurant. FILEY sits on the settee smoking a cigarette, casually turning over the pages of a magazine. The rifle is on the table.

There is a pause.

REG: They can't be long now, surely to God …!

FILEY tosses the magazine aside and takes a comb from his pocket.

FILEY: (*Combing his hair*) That's what you said ten minutes ago – twenty minutes ago – and if memory doesn't fail me, thirty minutes ago, Mr Bryer.

REG: Yes, well, I thought they'd have been out by now, otherwise … (*Suddenly; tensely*) Filey! Here they are! They're coming out!

REG quickly opens the window as FILEY springs into action, reaching for the rifle.

CUT TO: Outside the Positano Restaurant.

CAROL has emerged from the restaurant, onto the pavement and is waiting for HARRY. He suddenly appears in the background, adjusting his overcoat. He moves to CAROL who is now standing near the kerb.

CUT TO: The living room of Flat 19A Fulton Court.

FILEY is kneeling down by the open window, focussing the rifle on HARRY BRENT. REG stands watching him, tense and nervous. We see HARRY through the telescopic sight of the rifle. Suddenly the view of HARRY is completely obscured.

FILEY: (*Angry*) What the hell!

A large van has stopped in front of the restaurant. Only the back of the DRIVER's head can be seen as he talks to someone. CAROL and HARRY are no longer in view, being completely hidden by the van.

REG: It's all right, he'll be gone in a minute – he's only asking the way somewhere.

After a moment, the van pulls away. FILEY slowly raises the rifle to his shoulder but now the pavement is deserted. FILEY lowers the rifle. REG takes hold of his arm. They are both staring in bewilderment at the pavement opposite.

REG: What's happened? What the hell happened?

FILEY: They were tipped off.

CUT TO: The entrance hall of the Positano Restaurant. *HARRY and CAROL have re-entered the hall. HARRY is talking to a waiter. A tense and bewildered CAROL stands in the background watching HARRY. The WAITER appears somewhat confused by the conversation.*

WAITER: (*Pointing*) … But that's the main entrance, sir. If you turn left when you get into Fulton Street you'll …

HARRY: (*With authority*) I've told you, we don't want to use the main entrance! (*Producing a pound note*) Now be a good chap, take us out the back way.

WAITER: Er – yes, sir. Follow me, please … Madam …

HARRY turns and without looking at CAROL takes her by the arm.

CAROL: Harry, wait a minute! (*Trying to release her arm*) What happened just now?

HARRY looks at her; he is tense, faintly agitated.

CAROL: What did Mark say? Why was he driving that van?

HARRY: There was someone waiting for me … with a rifle … he was in the building opposite. Mark found out about it and … Carol, I'm sorry, but I just can't explain now! Come along!

CUT TO: A street near the restaurant.

HARRY's E-type Jaguar is parked in this street. The van suddenly turns into the street from the main road – it brakes to a standstill near the Jaguar. MARK RAINER climbs out of the driving seat and runs across to the Jaguar.

CUT TO: Staff Entrance to the Positano Restaurant. *HARRY and CAROL come out, then look along the street and dodge back against the wall. The Jaguar comes round the corner and stops nearby. RAINER switches off the car, gets out and walks to where CAROL and HARRY are waiting.*

RAINER: Here's the car, Harry. I'll see you later.

HARRY: Right! And thank you, Mark.

RAINER: Don't use this place again.

HARRY nods. RAINER glances at CAROL, then hesitatingly turns towards HARRY again.

RAINER: You've got a problem, Harry.

HARRY: Yes, I know – but I can handle it.

RAINER: (*Perturbed*) I hope so.

CAROL looks at the two men. She is not sure whether they are talking about her or not.

HARRY: Don't worry.

RAINER: I hope you can handle it, Harry, because if you can't then I just don't know what …

HARRY: (*Slightly annoyed*) It's my problem, Mark – don't worry! (*Relenting*) Who was it tonight? Filey?

RAINER: Yes. We were tipped off, thank God. I'll phone you later, Harry!

RAINER looks at CAROL, is obviously about to say something, then changes his mind and hurries away.

HARRY: Come on, Carol.

CAROL doesn't move from where she is standing.

CAROL: Did – did someone really try to kill you just now?

HARRY: (*Quietly*) Yes.

CAROL: Who?

HARRY: (*After a moment; watching CAROL*) A man called Filey. He was in the building opposite the restaurant. He had a rifle …

CAROL: (*Softly; incredulously*) Is this true, Harry?

HARRY: Yes, it's true.

120

CAROL: But why? Why should anyone want to kill you?

HARRY hesitates.

CAROL: Harry, you've got to tell me!

HARRY: Filey thinks I know something …

CAROL: About what?

HARRY: About – someone in Market Weldon …

CAROL: (*Puzzled*) Someone in Market Weldon?

HARRY: (*Taking hold of CAROL*) Look, we can't talk about this now! Let's go back to my place and then we can …

CAROL: (*With almost a suggestion of fear in her voice, trying to break away*) No. No, Harry …

HARRY: (*Apparently hurt by her refusal*) Carol, please!

CAROL stops struggling.

HARRY: (*Softly*) I didn't want to tell you this, but – I've had one hell of a day, darling. Please come back to the flat.

CAROL looks at him, hesitantly. He draws her towards him.

HARRY: If you come back with me I'll tell you about tonight. I'll tell you about Fielding, about Barbara Smith, (*Holding her closer*) I'll explain everything to you, Carol.

CAROL is bewildered, confused – not at all sure what to do. HARRY forces her to look at him.

CAROL: (*With a little nod*) All right, Harry.

CUT TO: The living room of HARRY BRENT's flat. Chelsea.

This is a well-furnished bachelor room, the room of a man with good taste and a reasonable amount of money. There are two doors, one leading into a bedroom, the other into the hall. The hall door is kept open.

HARRY is standing in front of an antique drinks table carefully mixing what appears to be a large dry martini.

121

There are various bottles and glasses on the table, also a telephone. HARRY is obviously taking a great deal of care over the mixing of this particular drink, stirring it well, adding just the right amount of vermouth. The bedroom door opens and CAROL enters. She looks tense, but less worried than in the previous scene. As she enters the room she replaces her lipstick in her handbag, HARRY turns and slowly crosses to her with the drink.

HARRY: Do you feel better now?

CAROL nods.

HARRY: Well, drink this.

CAROL takes the glass.

HARRY: Then we'll talk …

CAROL drinks, then sits on the settee. HARRY gets himself a whisky and soda. CAROL drinks again, then her head slumps, and her hand with the glass falls limply over the arm of the settee. HARRY turns and looks at her.

END OF EPISODE FOUR

EPISODE FIVE

TOLLY CHANGES HIS MIND

OPEN TO: The living room of HARRY BRENT's flat.

Harry dials a number on the telephone. The receiver is lifted at the other end and we suddenly hear MARK RAINER's voice.

RAINER: Sloane eight three six one …

HARRY: Mark, this is Harry.

CUT TO: *MARK RAINER is wearing a dressing-gown and is standing by a small bedside table. For the rest of this conversation, we cut back and forth between RAINER and HARRY.*

RAINER: Harry, where are you?

HARRY: I'm at the flat. I want to see you, Mark. Come round as soon as you can and bring the van – that's important.

RAINER: (*Puzzled*) Why do you want the van?

HARRY: I'll tell you when I see you.

RAINER: All right, I'll come round straight away. You sound worried, Harry.

HARRY: I am worried! Hellishly worried! Can you get hold of Jacqueline for me?

RAINER: What time is it? (*He looks at his watch*) I doubt whether she's back from the theatre yet.

HARRY: Well, try and get hold of her, Mark. I think she can help me.

HARRY replaces the receiver and stands for a second or two, deep in thought. Then he looks across the room towards the settee where CAROL has collapsed after taking the drink he prepared for her. The empty glass is on the floor. It is difficult to tell whether CAROL is dead – or asleep.

CUT TO: The living room of ALAN MILTON's flat.

The front doorbell is ringing and has been ringing for some considerable time. ALAN emerges from the bedroom in his pyjamas, hastily pulling on a dressing gown as he crosses towards the hall. About 5am.

ALAN: (*Calling*) All right! All right, I'm coming!

ALAN opens the front door and finds himself facing a tired and desperately agitated ERIC VYNER.

ALAN: (*Surprised*) Eric! At this time of the morning? What on earth …?

ERIC: Can I come in, Alan?

ALAN: Yes, of course! What is it? What's happened?

ERIC: (*Entering the hall*) I'm awfully sorry – getting you out of bed like this … I do apologise.

ALAN: (*Nodding towards the living room*) That's all right, Eric.

ERIC moves to the living room, turning towards ALAN as he does so.

ERIC: I'm worried, Alan – terribly worried!

ALAN: You don't have to be a detective to spot that. What are you worried about?

ERIC: I'm sure something's happened to Carol. She went up to London last night and hasn't returned.

ALAN: Perhaps she stayed the night in Town?

ERIC: No, she didn't, Alan! That's just the point! I've spoken to Harry – he put her on the train.

ALAN: (*Looking at ERIC*) Which train?

ERIC: The last one – the eleven-thirty. I met the train – I told her I was going to – but she wasn't on it.

ALAN: Well, perhaps she fell asleep on the train. That happens sometimes. That particular train goes on to Dalesbury.

ERIC: Yes, I know it does. I've just come from there. It stopped at Middleton, Roxby, Market Weldon, Railsford, and then Dalesbury. I've checked every station! (*Shaking his head*) She wasn't on the train, Alan!

126

ALAN speaks after a moment, realising that this might be a serious development.

ALAN: All right, let's start at the beginning. When did you last see her?

ERIC: Yesterday afternoon; I popped into the office for a few minutes. She caught the six-forty-five, had dinner with Harry at the Positano, then apparently he took her …

ALAN: The Positano?

ERIC: Yes, it's a little restaurant in Bloomsbury. Harry's very fond of it; he goes there quite a lot.

ALAN: (*Quietly*) Go on, Eric.

ERIC: After dinner – according to Harry – he drove her to the station. They were a few minutes early so they sat in his car for a while talking.

ALAN: Then what happened?

ERIC: He put her on the train. At least, that's what he says.

ALAN: Don't you believe him?

ERIC: (*Agitatedly*) Yes, of course I believe him!

ALAN: (*Quietly*) But – ?

ERIC: Well, if she was on the train, what the devil happened to her?

ALAN produces a pencil and notebook from a drawer.

ALAN: What was she wearing?

ERIC: Oh, God … (*Thoughtfully*) Now let me think …

ALAN: Did she change at the office?

ERIC: Yes, but I know what she was wearing … She had a dark blue dress on … You probably remember the dress, it had little red spots on it …

ALAN: Yes, I remember it. (*Writing*) I should. I bought it for her.

ERIC: And I think she had a fur stole with her – the one I gave her for Christmas. You've seen it, Alan.

127

ALAN: Was she wearing a hat? (*He answers his own question*) I shouldn't think so …

ERIC: No …

ALAN nods and continues writing

ALAN: (*Not looking up*) What did Harry say when you told him she wasn't on the train?

ERIC: He was bewildered, he just couldn't understand it. (*He looks at his watch*) Incidentally, I promised to ring him back. He's waiting for a call. Can I use your phone?

ALAN: Yes, go ahead. I'll get dressed.

ERIC speaks as ALAN moves towards the bedroom.

ERIC: Alan, what do you think happened to Carol?

ALAN: I don't know. I hope nothing's happened to her, Eric. (*Indicating phone*) Tell Harry Brent I want to see him. Ask him to be in my office at nine o'clock.

ALAN goes into the bedroom. ERIC crosses to the phone and dials a number. After a moment we hear the number ringing out at the other end. There is a pause. ERIC looks at the receiver, obviously surprised that there is no reply by now.

ALAN's VOICE: What's happened?

ERIC: There doesn't seem to be any reply …

ALAN: I should try again – perhaps you've dialled the wrong number.

ERIC hesitates, then replaces the receiver and dials again.

CUT TO: The living room of HARRY BRENT's flat.

The telephone is ringing. HARRY enters from the hall. He is wearing a coat and looks both agitated and faintly out of breath. He crosses to the phone, stares at it for a moment, then suddenly reaches out and picks up the receiver. For the rest of this conversation we cut back and forth between HARRY and ERIC.

HARRY: Hello?

ERIC: Harry?

HARRY: Yes – who is that?

ERIC: (*Puzzled by HARRY's manner*) This is Eric...

HARRY: I'm sorry, Eric. I didn't recognise your voice.

ERIC: You sound out of breath ...

HARRY: Yes, I am. I was downstairs, I ... Is there any news?

ERIC: (*Still puzzled by HARRY's manner*) No, I'm afraid there isn't. I take it you haven't heard anything? Carol hasn't phoned you, by any chance?

HARRY: No, I haven't heard a word from her. (*More composed*) I've been thinking, Eric. I suppose she could have fallen asleep. That train probably goes to Dalesbury...

ERIC: It does, but I've been there. I've checked every station. Look, Harry – there's something very odd about this.

HARRY: What do you mean, Eric – odd?

ERIC: Well, if she was on the train, she must have got off at one of the stations otherwise ... (*Stops, looking towards the bedroom. ALAN is in the doorway*)

ALAN: Don't forget I want to see him ...

ERIC: (*Nodding*) Yes, all right, Alan ...

HARRY: Who is that, Eric? Who are you talking to?

ERIC: I'm talking to Alan. I'm with him at the moment. I'm in his flat.

HARRY: Put him on. I'd like a word with him.

ERIC: (*To ALAN: offering him the receiver*) He wants to have a word with you, Alan.

ALAN hesitates, then shakes his head.

ALAN: Tell him to be in my office by nine o'clock. I'll talk to him then.

ALAN goes back into the bedroom. ERIC is faintly surprised by ALAN's attitude: he looks at the receiver.

ERIC: (*On phone*) He says he'll talk to you later, Harry.

HARRY: (*Surprised and irritated*) What does he mean – he'll talk to me later?

ERIC: That's what he said, Harry. He wants to see you in his office at nine o'clock.

HARRY: (*After a moment*) Okay. Tell the Inspector I'll be there. Nine o'clock. See you, Eric.

HARRY replaces the receiver then stands staring down at it, deep in thought.

CUT TO: The main entrance to Becklehurst Farm.

A police car approaches. ALAN is sitting in the back of the car. As the car slows down a second car – a Ford Zodiac complete with trailer – comes out of the very long drive leading up to the farm. The Ford is driven by HAROLD TOLLY. ALAN suddenly looks up and sees TOLLY staring at him; TOLLY gives a brief nod of recognition as his car turns into the main road. As the police car proceeds up the drive ALAN turns and looks back at the disappearing Ford.

CUT TO: Becklehurst Farm.

The police car draws into the courtyard and as ALAN climbs out of the back seat ERIC comes running out of the house to meet him.

ERIC: Is there any news of Carol?

ALAN: We've found her handbag, Eric – and shoes.

ERIC: (*Alarmed*) Where?

ALAN: A little girl found them, near the river, at Kingston.

ERIC: (*Softly*) Oh, my God … (*He turns away. Bitterly*) I'm going to get the car – I'm going over there!

ALAN: Eric, wait a minute! (*Restraining ERIC*) I've just come from Kingston. Believe me, there's no point in going there – there's absolutely nothing you can do.

ERIC: (*Dejected*) All right, Alan – if you say so ...

ALAN: Did you see Harry this morning?

ERIC: No, and I just can't understand it. Naturally, I was expecting him to call in, but he didn't. He didn't even phone me! Has he gone back to Town?

ALAN: (*Thoughtfully*) Yes, I imagine so. Eric, according to Harry, he and Carol had a row last night. They were both very upset, they broke things off ...

ERIC: (*Astonished*) I didn't know that ...

ALAN: (*Looking at ERIC*) That's what I wanted to ask you. Didn't Harry mention the row, when you spoke to him on the phone?

ERIC: No, he didn't ...

ALAN: You're sure?

ERIC: Yes, I'm quite sure.

ALAN: Thank you, Eric. Now don't worry; the moment I hear anything I'll get in touch with you.

ALAN crosses towards the car, then hesitates, and turns.

ALAN: (*Casually*) Was that Harold Tolly I saw driving out of the gate just now?

ERIC is deep in thought, pondering on what ALAN has just told him. He looks up, suddenly realising he has been asked a question.

ERIC: Tolly? ... Oh, yes ... He's looking for some plants for a stall of his. He thought I might be able to help him.

ALAN: Did you tell him about Carol?

ERIC: I said I was worried because she hadn't arrived home last night. Did I make a mistake? Shouldn't I have mentioned it?

ALAN: (*Unconcerned*) It doesn't matter, Eric.
ALAN gets into the car.

CUT TO: Outside C.I.D. Headquarters.
The police car draws up to the kerb and ALAN jumps out and hurries up the path towards the building. As he goes through the door we see that HAROLD TOLLY's Ford is parked on the opposite side of the road.

CUT TO: The Entrance Hall of C.I.D.
This hall is occasionally used as a waiting room; there are several chairs and a padded bench seat against the far wall. Doors lead to offices. There is a door marked "Gentlemen".
ALAN enters the hall as PHILIPS emerges from one of the offices carrying a sheaf of papers. As the two men stand talking a uniformed sergeant comes out of the "Gents" and goes into one of the offices.

ALAN: Hello, Roy! Any news from Kingston?
PHILIPS: No, nothing. I've just been onto them as a matter of fact. Eric Vyner called, he waited about half an hour in the hope ...
ALAN: (*Nodding*) I've seen Eric.
PHILIPS: There's been a call from Dalesbury, the Jason case comes up at two-thirty, not three o'clock ...
ALAN: That means we shall have to leave here about half past one.
PHILIPS: Yes. (*Suddenly*) Oh, by the way, Mr Tolly's here – he wants to see you.
ALAN: (*Surprised*) Tolly? But I've just seen him.
PHILIPS: To talk to?
ALAN: No; he was leaving Eric's place as we arrived. He must have come straight here. What does he want, do you know?
PHILIPS: He wouldn't say; he insists on seeing you.

132

ALAN crosses towards his office.

CUT TO: ALAN MILTON's Office.

HAROLD TOLLY is sitting in the armchair glancing through the pages of a magazine as he waits for ALAN. He wears a pin-stripe suit and the usual buttonhole. TOMLINS, the police clerk, is busy at the desk. As ALAN enters, TOLLY puts down the magazine and gets out of the chair.

ALAN: You want to see me?

TOLLY: Yes, if you can spare me a few minutes, Inspector?

ALAN: (*To TOMLINS*) All right. Leave us.

TOMLINS: Yes, sir.

He goes out. ALAN crosses to his desk

ALAN: I'm afraid it will only have to be a few minutes, Mr Tolly. I've a very busy day ahead of me.

TOLLY takes a postcard size photograph out of his inside pocket.

TOLLY: I did a spot of clearing up last night, went through some of Phyllis's – my wife's things. I found this photograph in an old handbag of hers. I thought perhaps you might be interested in it.

ALAN looks at TOLLY, then takes the photograph from him. We see that the photograph is of PHYLLIS TOLLY walking down Regent Street arm in arm with ERIC VYNER. Their heads are very close together in intimate conversation and they are both obviously unaware of the photographer.

ALAN: (*Looking at TOLLY again*) Have you shown this to anyone else?

TOLLY: No …

ALAN: You didn't show it to Mr Vyner?

TOLLY: No, I've told you, I haven't shown it to anyone … Oh, I see what you're getting at. (*Shaking his head*) I didn't see Vyner this morning because of the photograph.

ALAN: Why did you see him?

TOLLY: I need some plants and I was hoping he might be able to help me.

ALAN nods and looks at the photograph again.

ALAN: Did you know he was a friend of your wife's?

TOLLY: Well, I knew that he knew Phyllis, of course … He met her through his sister. But that photo seems to indicate that they were <u>very</u> good friends.

ALAN: (*Thoughtfully*) Yes. Yes, it does. (*Suddenly dismissing him*) Well, thank you, Mr Tolly, I'll keep this if I may?

TOLLY: (*Hesitant: surprised by the dismissal*) Yes, of course.

ALAN: (*After a moment*) Is there anything else you wanted to see me about?

TOLLY: Yes, there is. I've changed my mind.

ALAN: Changed your mind, Mr Tolly?

TOLLY: Yes. (*Embarrassed; hesitatingly*) I've decided to tell you the truth. It was perfectly true what Mrs Green told you the other day. I did ask her to get the pen for me – Fielding's pen. I offered her fifty pounds for it.

TOLLY takes FIELDING's pen out of his pocket and puts it on the desk. ALAN quietly watches him.

ALAN: Why did you want the pen?

TOLLY: A man I know asked me to get it for him – he said he'd … pay a lot of money for it …

ALAN: What do you call a lot of money?

TOLLY: Four hundred pounds. Cash.

ALAN: Who was this man?

134

TOLLY hesitates.

ALAN: Was it the man we picked up – Kevin Jason?

TOLLY: Yes …

ALAN: How well do you know Jason?

TOLLY: I hardly know him at all. He introduced himself to me one night; in The Crown at Kingston. He said he understood my wife was a friend of Mrs Green's. We stood talking for a little while; he bought me a couple of drinks. I thought he was a bit of a "nut". I didn't take him too seriously. But he was in the pub the next night and we got talking again. That's when he put the proposition up to me.

ALAN: Did he tell you why he wanted the pen? Why he was prepared to pay so much for it?

TOLLY: No, he didn't. I asked him. He said that was his business. My business was to get the pen. I still think he's a "nut" – that damn thing isn't worth a fiver.

ALAN: Why didn't you tell me about this before, Tolly?

TOLLY: I didn't want to get into trouble. Besides …

ALAN: Go on …

TOLLY: Jason paid me two hundred quid on account. I thought I might lose it if – if it told you what had really happened.

ALAN: I see.

TOLLY: *(Rising)* I've – I've told you the truth, Inspector. I'm only sorry I didn't tell you it before.

ALAN comes round the desk, joining TOLLY.

ALAN: So am I, Mr Tolly.

TOLLY: *(His self-confidence returning; smiling)* Well – I've given you some information, now perhaps you'll give me some.

ALAN: (*Crossing to the door*) What is it you want to know?

TOLLY: What did Jason tell you? What was <u>his</u> story?

ALAN: He refuses to talk; he won't tell us anything.

TOLLY: Refuses … (*Surprised*) Are you still holding him, then?

ALAN: Yes; he broke into my flat a few days ago. He was armed, and he threatened me. The case comes up this afternoon.

TOLLY: I didn't know that! Well, I'm damned! So that's why you picked him up!

ALAN opens the door.

ALAN: That's right, Mr Tolly. Now if you'll excuse me, sir.

PHILIPS appears in the open doorway: he obviously wishes to speak to ALAN – but not in front of TOLLY.

TOLLY: Yes, of course. (*He hesitates, as if about to say something else, then changes his mind*) Good morning, Inspector.

ALAN: Good morning, sir.

TOLLY nods to PHILIPS and goes out. PHILIPS enters the office, closing the door behind him.

PHILIPS: There's been a message through from Jason …

ALAN: (*Surprised*) Jason?

PHILIPS: He wants to see you before the case comes up. They're bringing him here at twelve o'clock.

ALAN: (*Looking at PHILIPS; intrigued*) Is he going to talk, Roy?

PHILIPS: (*Smiling*) Yes, I think he is.

CUT TO: Outside C.I.D. Headquarters.

A police car arrives and KEVIN JASON gets out of the car accompanied by LAIDMAN and STONE, two plain clothes men. The three men walk towards the building.

CUT TO: The Entrance Hall of C.I.D.

JASON enters followed by the two detectives. LAIDMAN takes JASON to the bench seat as the other man crosses to ALAN's office. STONE knocks on the door, then enters the office, closing the door behind him.

JASON: (*To LAIDMAN: with a touch of sarcasm*) Would you think it presumptuous of me, if I requested permission to use the John?

LAIDMAN: (*Smiling*) Go ahead …

JASON rises and crosses towards the door marked "Gentlemen". LAIDMAN follows him.

LAIDMAN: (*As JASON opens the door*) You'll never make it. Tom Thumb couldn't climb out of that window.

JASON looks at him, unsmiling, and makes a rude gesture with his fingers as he goes into the toilet. LAIDMAN smiles: glances at his watch. A uniformed sergeant appears and nods to LAIDMAN as he leaves the building. ALAN's door opens and STONE appears in the doorway.

STONE: (*To LAIDMAN*) Okay – the Inspector's free now.

LAIDMAN: (*Nodding towards the toilet door*) He won't be a minute. I'll bring him in.

STONE nods and goes back into the office closing the door behind him.

CUT TO: The small Gents lavatory in C.I.D. Headquarters.

KEVIN JASON is standing on the lavatory seat searching for something which has apparently been placed on top of the old-fashioned cistern. He suddenly finds the object he is looking for – it is a gun. A slip of paper has been attached to the gun by means of Sellotape. JASON quickly opens the note and looks at it. We see the typed note reads: "Will pick you up Clarence Gate Richmond Park". JASON puts the note in his pocket then turns towards the door – he is tensed up, ready for action.

CUT TO: The Entrance Hall of C.I.D. Headquarters. *LAIDMAN is still waiting for KEVIN JASON to come out of the "Gents". A uniformed policewoman appears carrying a heavy typewriter and crosses towards one of the offices.*

LAIDMAN: Hello, Sylvia! Don't tell me they're making you work for a living these days?

SYLVIA: No, I always do this in the coffee break!

LAIDMAN smiles to himself as the girl disappears into an office. The door behind him opens and JASON appears.

LAIDMAN: (*Turning*) Okay – the Inspector's ready now.

JASON doesn't answer, but suddenly moves nearer LAIDMAN, standing very close to him. LAIDMAN quickly looks down. The Irishman has the gun in his hand.

LAIDMAN: (*Frightened*) Where the hell did you get that from?

JASON: (*Tensely*) Now listen – one squeak out of you and by God you've had it!

LAIDMAN doesn't know what to do: he glances across at ALAN's office, hoping the door will open.

JASON: Walk towards the street with me …

LAIDMAN hesitates.

JASON: You heard – take me to the door!

LAIDMAN is still undecided what to do.

JASON: (*Intensely angry*) I shall use this bloody thing! I'm warning you!

LAIDMAN appears to be really frightened now: he moves across to the entrance with JASON by his side. Just as they reach the entrance to the street ALAN's door opens and PHILIPS appears. LAIDMAN springs towards JASON in a desperate attempt to take advantage of the situation and get the gun. The Irishman is too quick for him – he fires. As the

138

detective staggers back clutching his stomach, JASON rushes out of the building and into the street. PHILIPS quickly crosses to LAIDMAN as office doors are thrown open and people pour into the hall. ALAN is one of the first on the scene followed by the bewildered DETECTIVE STONE.

CUT TO: Outside C.I.D. Headquarters.
KEVIN JASON is running hell-for-leather down the street towards the main road.

CUT TO: Outside Putney Underground Station.
A train has just arrived, and people are rushing out of the station. KEVIN JASON can be seen hurrying towards the nearest bus stop, trying to make himself as inconspicuous as possible.

CUT TO: An entrance to Richmond Park (Clarence Gate)
JASON is pacing up and down in front of the entrance to the park. He looks tense and extremely worried. It is obvious that he is waiting to be picked up by someone – and the friend is late. A van appears at the end of the road and JASON watches it with interest as it approaches the park. Suddenly, to the Irishman's annoyance, it turns off the road and goes down a side street.
JASON continues pacing up and down, ignoring the private cars which appear – he is obviously expecting a van. After a little while another van appears at the far end of the road and continues towards the park. JASON watches it; keyed up.
As the van draws nearer we see that it is being driven by REG BRYER and that there is a name-sign on the side of the vehicle, "Westdown Laundry". The Irishman's face breaks into a relieved smile. The van slackens speeds and crawls past JASON but doesn't actually stop. Surprised by this JASON starts running towards the van, his eyes on the rear shutters

(roller shutters, not doors) which are closed. Across the shutters are painted the words "Westdown Laundry". Suddenly the shutters are opened, and we see a grim faced FILEY standing inside the van. He is holding the rifle with the telescopic sight. JASON stops running, obviously bewildered and frightened by the sight of the man inside the van. FILEY raises the rifle to his shoulder and fires. The Irishman, hit by the bullet, staggers backwards in the road. There is a second shot as JASON slumps to the ground. FILEY lowers the rifle, and leaning forward, quickly closes the shutter. The van gathers speed as KEVIN JASON's body lies in the road.

CUT TO: Outside the Westminster Club, St James's Street, London.
A taxi pulls up at the entrance to this famous old club. HARRY BRENT gets out of the cab and, after paying the driver, starts to take off his hat and coat as he walks into the building.

CUT TO: The lobby of the Westminster Club.
CLAYTON, the Head Porter, is in his private "cubby-hole" reading a newspaper. HARRY walks into the lobby carrying his hat and coat.

HARRY: Good afternoon.
CLAYTON: (*Looking up*) Good afternoon, sir.
HARRY: Sir Gordon Town's expecting me.
CLAYTON: Yes, of course, sir. Mr Brent?
HARRY: That's right.
CLAYTON comes out of his office.
CLAYTON: Please come this way, sir. I'll take your hat and coat, if I may, sir?
HARRY hands over his hat and coat
HARRY: Thank you.

CUT TO: A corner of the Smoking Room, Westminster Club.

SIR GORDON TOWN is sitting in an armchair enjoying a glass of sherry. He is a tall, shrewdly casual man in his late fifties. HARRY arrives with CLAYTON.

CLAYTON: Mr Brent, sir.

TOWN: Ah! Thank you, Clayton.

TOWN rises as CLAYTON returns to the lobby.

TOWN: Nice to see you, Brent. (*They shake hands*) How are you?

HARRY: I'm very well, thank you, sir – considering.

TOWN indicates the other armchair.

TOWN: Do sit down.

As HARRY sits, a WAITER appears.

TOWN: What would you like – a glass of sherry?

HARRY: May I have a dry martini?

TOWN: Can we manage a dry martini, Derek?

WAITER: We'll do our best, sir.

The WAITER goes.

TOWN: Before I forget, Brent. The Doctor wants to see you – Thursday next, three o'clock.

HARRY: (*Rather surprised and irritated*) But I had a check-up, four months ago!

TOWN: Yes, I know. But you know Morgan – he practically runs the department these days. He's tiresomely conscientious, I'm afraid.

HARRY: (*Annoyed*) Look, sir – please tell Morgan there's nothing the matter with my health! Believe me, when I feel I can't do this job I shall be the very first to …

TOWN: You tell him, Brent. You're so much better at that sort of thing than I am. (*Smiling*) However, we didn't meet to discuss your reflexes, excellent though I'm sure they are,

141

	my dear fellow. I gather from Rainer you have a problem?
HARRY:	Yes, sir.
TOWN:	Is it the girl?
HARRY:	Partly ... (*Quickly*) But I take full responsibility for that, sir.
TOWN:	(*Smiles*) Well – if it's not Miss Vyner – what is it?
HARRY:	(*Quietly, leaving forward*) This business is coming to a head – with a bit of luck we'll be picking the bastard up in a day or two.
TOWN:	Well?
HARRY:	I'd like to tell Alan Milton about Fielding; I'd like to tell him the whole story.
TOWN:	Alan Milton? He's the local man – the Inspector?
HARRY:	Yes. Have I your permission, sir?
TOWN:	Do you think it's necessary to tell him the whole story, Brent?
HARRY:	Yes, I do. He's intelligent, he's on the ball, and he's highly conscientious.
TOWN:	Oh dear; he sounds exactly like Morgan.
HARRY:	If we don't put him in the picture I think there'll be trouble, sir.
TOWN:	What kind of trouble?
HARRY:	Well – supposing he makes an arrest, at the wrong moment?
TOWN:	(*Nodding*) Yes, that's a point to consider, I suppose.
HARRY:	Besides, he's got some information I want. Oh, I know you can get it for me, you can go at the A.C. if necessary. But things are hotting up and at any moment now we may need his

	help – and we may need it on the spur of the moment, sir.
TOWN:	And what about Miss Vyner? Do you want to put her into the picture too?
HARRY:	That's up to you, sir.
TOWN:	Yes, I thought you'd say that. Is that what you'd call accepting responsibility?
HARRY:	(*Annoyed*) You seem to forget – the girl was your idea.
TOWN:	I asked you to get friendly with her – that was all.
HARRY:	I did get friendly with her.
TOWN:	Yes, but unfortunately that <u>wasn't</u> all, was it, Brent?
HARRY:	(*Ignoring the remark*) Well, have I your permission? Do I talk to Milton?
TOWN:	If you talk to Milton you might just as well talk to the girl; you know that as well as I do.
HARRY:	Yes, sir.
TOWN:	You'd have to tell her the whole story, right from the beginning.
HARRY:	Yes, sir.
TOWN:	Is that what you want, Brent?
HARRY:	(*Bluntly*) Yes, it is. I think it's about time I was frank with her. It'll make a nice change, if nothing else.

TOWN looks at HARRY, there is the suggestion of a smile on his face.

TOWN:	We do have our problems, don't we, Brent?
HARRY:	(*Depressed*) I take it the answer's no?

There is another pause, then TOWN leans forward and pats HARRY's arm

| TOWN: | My dear fellow, you really mustn't jump to conclusions. You know what you, and your |

> friends in the department, always say about
> me. Completely unpredictable.

HARRY looks at TOWN.

TOWN: We'll talk about it over lunch.

CUT TO: The living room of JACQUELINE DAWSON's flat, Esher, Surrey.

JACQUELINE DAWSON lives in a small and somewhat exclusive block of flats near Esher Common. The rooms are light and airy; the furnishings pleasant – if a shade theatrical. *Through a half-open-door JACQUELINE can be seen working in a modern kitchen. Various doors lead to bedrooms, entrance hall, etc. The phone rings and JACQUELINE comes out of the kitchen and crosses to the telephone which stands next to a tape-recorder on a table.*

JACQUELINE: (*On phone*) Esher six eight nine 0 one.

CUT TO: Interior of a telephone box.

For the rest of this conversation we cut back and forth between the telephone box and JACQUELINE DAWSON's living room.

HARRY: Jacqueline! This is Harry!
JACQUELINE: Harry, where are you? Where are you speaking from?
HARRY: I'm in a phone box. I'm on my way out to you – I'll be there in twenty minutes.
JACQUELINE: How did the lunch go?
HARRY: It wasn't easy – but I got what I wanted. How are things at your end?

CUT TO: The living room of JACQUELINE DAWSON's flat. As before.

JACQUELINE is still speaking on the phone.

144

JACQUELINE: Oh, it's still the same mad little get together! But there's nothing to worry about. Don't be too long, Harry.

JACQUELINE replaces the phone and after a slight hesitation takes a key from a box on the table and crosses to one of the bedrooms. Then she unlocks the bedroom door. CAROL is in the bedroom, standing near the door – she has obviously been listening to the phone conversation. She looks tired and angry; she is still wearing her evening dress, but she has kicked off her shoes and her fur stole is on the bed.

JACQUELINE: That was Harry on the phone. He's coming out to see you, he'll be here in twenty minutes. (*She turns, then hesitates*) Miss Vyner, I know this must be very difficult for you to believe, but we didn't keep you here last night without a very good reason.

CAROL: What was your reason?

JACQUELINE: Ask Harry, he'll tell you.

CAROL: I'm asking you, Miss Dawson! (*Intensely angry*) What happened last night? I want to know!

JACQUELINE: Harry gave you a drink; there was a sedative in it. A very strong one, I'm afraid. He wanted to make you sleepy so we could bring you down here, to Esher, without any fuss. You passed out on him. He was scared – really scared – at one time he thought you were dead.

CAROL: Yes, but why did he want to bring me here in the first place? I fail to see …

JACQUELINE: Someone tried to kill Harry last night – fortunately they failed. But Harry was worried, he felt sure they'd try to get at him

145

	again, perhaps in some other way – perhaps through you.
CAROL:	Through me?
JACQUELINE:	Yes, but they won't, not now – don't worry.
CAROL:	How do you know they won't?
JACQUELINE:	Because the gentleman in question happens to think you're dead, Miss Vyner. He thinks you committed suicide last night.

CUT TO: Roehampton Vale, London.

HARRY BRENT is in   his E-type Jaguar driving out towards Esher. It is about three-thirty in the afternoon. A van pulls onto the main road from a service station and for a moment causes a temporary hold-up. The van suddenly takes advantage of the situation and, gathering speed, races towards the Kingston By-Pass. HARRY manages to pass the rest of the   traffic but finally finds himself held up by the van itself which is now clearly "hogging" the centre of the road. The van refuses to move over and the Jaguar is compelled to slow down. Whilst HARRY curses to himself and impatiently waits for the driver of the van to give way, we have a view of the vehicle through the windscreen of the Jaguar. We can see, quite clearly, the words painted on the shutters at the rear of the van – "Westdown Laundry".

END OF EPISODE FIVE

EPISODE SIX
THE THIRD PERSON

OPEN TO: *HARRY Brent's E-type Jaguar continues to drive along Roehampton Vale behind the van marked "Westdown Laundry". A police car drives up behind them. It pulls out passing HARRY's car at a tremendous speed and braking to a standstill about twenty or thirty yards ahead of the van. Two UNIFORMED POLICEMEN jump out of the car and wave the van into the side of the road. HARRY pulls out and passes the van. He glances at the police as he goes by. The POLICEMEN go to the van and open the passenger side door. The driver of the van is Ben – a bald-headed man in his early forties. He looks bewildered.*

BEN: What's up?

1st POLICEMAN: Do you mind getting out, please? We'd like to take a look inside the van.

BEN: Okay.

BEN climbs out of the van and walks round to the rear. He opens the shutters of the van. The van is empty except for three large cardboard boxes marked "Westdown Laundry".

2nd POLICEMAN: Where are you going?

BEN: I'm going back to Westdown. I've just been delivering some stuff to Langham's.

2nd POLICEMAN: Langham's? The drapers – Putney High Street?

BEN: That's right. (*Puzzled*) I say, what is this?

2nd POLICEMAN: What's your name?

BEN: Armitage. Ben Armitage. Look – what's this all about?

The 1st POLICEMAN has been examining the van; he returns to BEN.

1st POLICEMAN: A man was shot near Richmond Park. Someone reported seeing a van – one like this – in the vicinity.

BEN: Strewth!

2nd POLICEMAN: Do you work for the Westdown Laundry?

BEN: Yes, and Fletcher's, the dry cleaners. It's
                       the same firm. I've been with them for
                       eight years.

2nd POLICEMAN: Let's see your licence and insurance
                       certificate.

*BEN feels in his pocket, and takes out a wallet, and produces
his driving licence and insurance certificate. The
POLICEMEN examine them.*

CUT TO: The living room of JACQUELINE DAWSON's
flat.

*JACQUELINE DAWSON is sitting in an armchair smoking a
cigarette and watching CAROL who is on the settee opposite
her. CAROL is tense and still very much "on edge". There
are tea things on a small table near the settee.*

JACQUELINE: Are you sure you wouldn't like another
                       cup of tea?

CAROL: Yes, I'm positive.

JACQUELINE: Well, please, do try to relax, Miss Vyner.
                       (*Smiling*) If it's only until Harry gets here.

CAROL: You said he'd be here in twenty minutes.

JACQUELINE: I did. And that was exactly – (*She looks at
                       her watch*) – twenty-four minutes ago.

*CAROL hesitates as if about to say something, then she leans
forward and picks up a cigarette from a box on the table. She
looks at the cigarette, then suddenly changes her mind and
tosses it back into the box. As she does so the phone rings.
JACQUELINE looks at the phone, then crosses the room and
answers it. CAROL turns and watches her, curious about the
call – wondering if it is HARRY again.*

JACQUELINE: (*On phone*) Esher six eight nine 0 one.

CUT TO: ALAN MILTON's Office.

ALAN is sitting at his desk, on the phone. For the rest of this conversation we cut back and forth between ALAN's office and JACQUELINE's flat.

ALAN: This is Inspector Milton. Can I speak to Mr Brent, please?

JACQUELINE: (*Surprised, glancing across at CAROL*) I'm sorry, he's not here just now, but I'm expecting him at any moment.

There is the sound of the front door opening and closing and both JACQUELINE and CAROL look towards the hall.

JACQUELINE: (*On phone*) Wait a second! I think he's just arrived.

HARRY enters from the hall. CAROL quickly rises from the settee; they stand looking at each other. JACQUELINE speaks to HARRY, indicating the phone.

JACQUELINE: This is for you. It's Inspector Milton …

CAROL: (*Surprised*) Alan!

She turns and is about to move towards the phone when HARRY stops her, quickly taking hold of her arm.

HARRY: Carol, please! (*To JACQUELINE*) I tried to get him an hour ago, but he was out. I left this number.

ALAN is still on the phone, puzzled by the delay. PHILIPS can now be seen in the background.

ALAN: Hello? … Hello? … (*To PHILIPS*) I don't know what the devil's going on here …

PHILIPS: Have they rung off?

ALAN: I don't think so …

PHILIPS: Who's number is that?

ALAN: I don't know. It's the number Harry Brent left. A woman answered the phone. (*Suddenly*) Hello?

HARRY: Inspector Milton – this is Harry Brent …

ALAN:	Oh, good afternoon! I have a message on my desk, asking me to ring you …
HARRY:	Yes, that's right, Inspector. I'd like to see you – some time this evening if possible.
ALAN:	What is it you want to see me about – Carol?
HARRY:	(*Ignoring the question*) Would eight o'clock be convenient, at your flat? I know the address.
ALAN:	(*After a moment; curious*) Yes, all right, Mr Brent. Eight o'clock.
HARRY:	Oh, and Inspector – would you be kind enough to phone … (*He takes a piece of paper from his pocket and glances at it*) Chief Superintendent Stenton at Scotland Yard; extension thirty-four …? Any time before six-thirty …
ALAN:	(*Surprised*) Superintendent Stenton?
HARRY:	Yes, he's expecting a call from you. I'll see you at eight o'clock, Mr Milton.

CUT TO: JACQUELINE DAWSON's living room. As before.

HARRY replaces the receiver and looks across at CAROL. She is standing next to JACQUELINE, puzzled and bewildered by the phone call. JACQUELINE is holding CAROL's arm, ready to restrain her from moving towards the phone. As HARRY moves towards the settee JACQUELINE relaxes her hold on CAROL.

CAROL:	Why do you want to see Alan? And why ask him to phone Scotland Yard? (*She looks at JACQUELINE, then at HARRY again*) Are – are you connected with the police?

152

HARRY:	Carol, have you heard of D.I. Five?
CAROL:	D.I. Five? No …?
HARRY:	Well, it is a Government agency. I work for it, so does Miss Dawson, and Mark Rainer. (*Indicates settee*) Please sit down, Carol. I want to tell you about Tom Fielding.

CAROL hesitates, then sits on the settee.

| HARRY: | (*Quietly; to JACQUELINE*) I'd like the Inspector to hear this. |

JACQUELINE nods and, crossing to the tape-recorder, switches it on.

HARRY:	Some time ago Tom Fielding told the Ministry of Aviation that he was working on a new radar device; a revolutionary improvement on anything we have at the present time. The Ministry investigated his claim, discovered that Fielding was in fact on to something very big, and asked him to continue his work under their supervision. Tom refused to do this. He insisted on working alone.
CAROL:	I can believe that.
HARRY:	Now this presented many difficulties. One or two people had heard of the invention and they tried, unsuccessfully of course, to do a deal with Fielding. About three months ago, the old boy received a communication from a Mr X – it was brief and to the point. It said if Tom wasn't prepared to do business with him, he'd be murdered.
JACQUELINE:	Unfortunately, Tom didn't take the warning seriously …

153

HARRY:	But we did – because although we didn't know the identity of X we did know the ruthless international set-up who were backing him. We knew that ultimately, if X couldn't get the invention, it would be in his interest to see that no one else got it. *(Moving nearer to CAROL)* I spent hours with Tom, trying to persuade him to leave Market Weldon and work at a Government hide-out. He refused – flatly refused to even consider the idea. (*He shrugs*) So, I'm afraid, we had no alternative but to try and watch him night and day. But it was an impossible task. You can't protect a man twenty-four hours a day unless he's really prepared to co-operate with you, and Tom Fielding wasn't.
JACQUELINE:	X knew that Harry and I were friendly with Fielding; and concluded that we were playing the same game as himself for some rival organisation.
HARRY:	He never dreamt, of course, that we were attached to D.I. Five. In fact, at the beginning, he just didn't know who the devil we were – that's why he had those films taken, in the hope of identifying us.
CAROL:	But what about Barbara Smith – the girl who shot Fielding? Was she working for X?
HARRY:	Her real name was Worthing. Barbara Worthing. She was a New Zealander; she came to this country – via the Continent – about four months ago. According to an agent of ours she was a drug addict. X had

heard of Barbara Worthing – in fact he knew a great deal about her – but she wasn't actually working for him.

JACQUELINE: When X finally decided to kill Tom Fielding, he made up his mind to throw suspicion on Harry. He told one of his men, a man called Filey, to get friendly with Barbara Worthing and introduce himself to her as Harry Brent. Naturally, the girl thought this was his name – she'd no reason to think otherwise.

HARRY: Filey's a killer; a ruthless character who'll do anything for money, but – God knows why – women always seem to fall for him.

JACQUELINE: You know what happened. She went to Market Weldon, visited the cemetery because Filey – "Harry Brent" – had asked her to, and then   …

CAROL: Yes, but surely she didn't shoot Fielding just because someone told her to?

JACQUELINE: She was mad about Filey; crazy about him. She was prepared to do anything he wanted. Besides – she desperately needed heroin, and Filey had promised to get it for her.

CAROL: Is this true, Harry?

HARRY: Yes, completely true. Except that I don't believe the girl really knew what she was doing. (*To JACQUELINE*) It's my opinion Filey told her the gun had blanks in it, and that the object of the exercise was simply to scare Fielding.

JACQUELINE: Well, you could be right, Harry – but I'm not sure.

CAROL: But what about the photograph – the one that was
         sent to the office?
HARRY: Our agent in Switzerland sent it. He'd heard that
         Fielding was advertising for a secretary and he
         sent the photograph as a warning, just in case
         Filey told Barbara Worthing to apply for the job.
CAROL: I see.

*CAROL nods, and thoughtfully rising from the settee, moves
towards the table. She stands looking at the tape-recorder.
There is a pause. HARRY glances across at JACQUELINE.*

HARRY: (*Quietly*) I know what you're thinking, Carol.
CAROL: Do you, Harry?
HARRY: You're wondering if that's why I got friendly with
         you – simply because you worked for Fielding.

CAROL turns.

HARRY: Well, the answer's yes. (*He moves towards
         CAROL*) Tom Fielding recommended my firm to
         you because I told him to. Because I told him it
         would probably be to his advantage, as well as
         mine, if I got to know you.
CAROL: Well, at least you're honest – if nothing else.
HARRY: Yes, but – unfortunately there was something I
         overlooked. I fell in love.

CAROL turns and looks at him.

CUT TO: The living room of ALAN MILTON's flat.
The tape recorder is playing back.
CAROL's VOICE:Did you fall in love with me, Harry?
*ALAN's hand comes into shot. He switches off the recorder.
He looks up at HARRY.*
HARRY: I don't blame you for suspecting me; X did a first-
         class job as far as throwing suspicion onto Harry
         Brent was concerned. The theatre tickets must
         have convinced you I knew the girl.

156

ALAN: Well, I must confess I was shaken when you had a ticket for the same show – the same night – the very next seat. Although I realised, of course, that the ticket could have been planted when the wallet was stolen. But tell me about Miss Dawson. Why did she send me that message?

HARRY: (*Smiling*) We wanted you to go to Kingsdown Mansions and find out about Mrs Tolly.

ALAN: But why were you interested in Mrs Tolly?

HARRY: (*Smiling*) That's a good question. She worked for X and she'd been tailing me – she'd been tailing me for some time. One night Fielding saw her in a coffee bar. I was with Tom; he spotted her just as she left.

ALAN: But she told me about that meeting.

HARRY: (*Smiling*) She told you her version of it. That's why we sent you to Richmond, we thought it was about time you knew a little more about her. We didn't realise of course that she was going to be murdered. (*He rises and crosses to the drinks table*) I went to Kingsdown Mansions the night it happened; I caught a glimpse of the murderer, unfortunately it was pretty dark, and I didn't recognise him. But he thinks I did. (*He puts his glass down on the table*) That's why I had to get Carol out of the way – even to the extent of making people think she'd committed suicide. I knew X would try and get back at me, if only through Carol.

ALAN: But why did you go to Kingsdown Mansions?

HARRY: I was curious about Reg Bryer, the caretaker. I had a hunch he was mixed up in this business, so I searched his flat. Incidentally, I was right. He's a friend of Filey's.

157

ALAN: (*Rising and moving to the table*) Tell me more about this – X, as you call him.

HARRY: There's nothing else I can tell you. We've beaten him, so far as Fielding is concerned – we collected all the data we wanted twenty-four hours before the poor old boy was shot. But we still don't know who X is.

ALAN: Does X know that you've got what you wanted?

HARRY: No; he thinks we haven't, and we've encouraged him to think that way.

ALAN: In the hope that he'd come out into the open?

HARRY: Yes. That was the idea of the pen – but it misfired, I'm afraid. After the murder, one of our people pretended he wanted to get hold of Tom's pen; he came down to Market Weldon and made discreet enquiries about it. He was inferring, of course, that the pen contained something of importance, relating to Tom's work. X wasn't taking any chances – within a matter of hours Tolly had contacted Mrs Green about it.

ALAN: But what was the idea – what did you think would happen?

HARRY: We thought that Tolly would hand the pen over to X: that's why Jacqueline and Mark Rainer were watching his stall that morning. (*He looks at his watch*) I'm afraid I must go. I promised Carol I'd drop in on Eric before I went back to Town.

ALAN: Does Eric know that Carol's safe and at Esher?

HARRY: No, he doesn't, and we don't want him to know. We don't want anyone to know. Not at the moment, at any rate.

ALAN: (*Quietly*) All right, if that's the way you want it.

HARRY nods, picks up his hat and coat from a chair, and crosses to the door.

158

HARRY: Good night, Inspector.

ALAN: Good night! (*As Harry opens the door*) Give Carol
my love.

HARRY turns.

HARRY: I will, Mr Milton. I will indeed.

HARRY goes out.

CUT TO: Becklehurst Farm. Night.

*HARRY's Jaguar arrives in the courtyard and stops near the
path leading up to the house. The house is in darkness and as
HARRY climbs out of the car he notices a light flashing from
one of the farm buildings. This is a large barn with a
corrugated roof; it stands about fifty yards or so away from
the house and is used mainly for storage. HARRY looks
towards the light and as he does so it flashes again and a
man's voice calls across to him from the doorway of the barn.*

VOICE: Mr Vyner will be with you in a minute, sir!

HARRY: (*Calling back*) Okay.

*HARRY takes a cigarette case and lighter out of his pocket.
He lights a cigarette and stands leaning against the car,
waiting for ERIC. After a while he glances at his watch,
stares across the courtyard, then decides to stroll towards the
barn in search of ERIC. As HARRY approaches the barn the
door can be seen to be half open. FILEY is in the barn,
standing just inside the doorway, waiting for HARRY. He
looks tense and alert; there is a gun in his hand. HARRY is
still walking towards the barn, but his pace has slackened, he
is slightly suspicious now – looking at the half open door with
curiosity. FILEY – gun in hand – is still waiting for HARRY to
enter the barn. HARRY is within about ten yards of the barn;
he is slowly approaching the doorway. He stops and picks up
several stones and holds them in his right hand. He suddenly
stops and raises his arm as if about to throw the stones onto
the corrugated tin roof. FILEY, keyed up and ready for*

159

action, watches the opening to the barn. The footsteps have stopped. FILEY waits, gun raised, suddenly, and apparently from behind him, there is a noisy continuous clatter. HARRY has tossed the stones onto the roofing at the rear of the building. FILEY is taken completely by surprise and, springing from his hiding place, turns suspiciously towards the bales of straw and discarded agricultural implements at the rear of the barn. HARRY takes immediate advantage of the situation; hurling himself through the doorway and bringing an astonished FILEY to the ground. The two men struggle for the gun – it is difficult to tell who is winning. The violent struggle continues – suddenly there is the sound of a shot, and FILEY staggers back against a bale of straw clutching his stomach. He falls to the ground. HARRY, breathless and exhausted stands looking down at FILEY. After a moment he kneels down and examines the dead man. He is about to rise when a shadow falls across the dead man. HARRY quickly turns but as he does so a knife is plunged into his chest. With a cry HARRY falls backwards onto the floor of the bar. He remains there, motionless – the knife is still in his body.

CUT TO: An alcove table in the Weldon Steak House. Night.
ALAN has finished his dinner and is thoughtfully drinking a cup of coffee. A WAITER comes to the table and puts down a plate with ALAN's change and receipt on it.
WAITER: Your change, sir.
ALAN: Thank you.
The WAITER goes away. ALAN is looking at the receipt, deciding on the amount to leave the WAITER, when he looks up and sees PHILIPS approaching the table.
ALAN: (*Surprised*) Hello, Roy!

PHILIPS: We've been looking all over the place for you! I
phoned your flat and when there was no reply …

ALAN: I do eat, occasionally you know … (*He stops,
looking at PHILIPS*) What is it, Roy? What's
happened?

PHILIPS looks round, then sits.

PHILIPS: It's Harry Brent – he's dead! He's been murdered!

ALAN: What! (*Stunned*) Dead … Are you sure?

PHILIPS: I've seen him! I've just left the doctor.

ALAN: But – he was with me, only an hour ago! He told
me he was going to see Eric and then drive back to
Town!

PHILIPS: (*Nodding*) It was Eric that found him. So far as I
can gather when he got to the farm Eric was out.
As a matter of fact …

ALAN: Look, start at the beginning. What happened –
how was he killed?

PHILIPS: He was knifed. Eric found him in the barn, the one
nearest the house. There was another man there, a
man called Filey. He was dead too, he'd been shot
through the stomach.

ALAN: What happened? What the hell happened, Roy?

PHILIPS: I think Harry Brent and Filey went for each other
and Filey was shot – then, at the last moment …

ALAN: Go on …

PHILIPS: This is just my opinion, it's just a theory …

ALAN: (*Tensely*) Go on …

PHILIPS: I think suddenly, at the very last moment someone
else – a third person – appeared on the scene …

ALAN: Yes … Yes, that makes sense!

PHILIPS: Eric told me he was expecting Harry but he had a
phone call from Harold Tolly and had to go into
Market Weldon. When he got back, he saw
Harry's car in the courtyard. He knew Harry

161

wasn't in the house because it was closed – the housekeeper's away for a couple of days. He looked all over the place, then eventually went down to the barn. My God, you can just imagine how he felt! Eric's shaken – really shaken.

ALAN: (*Suddenly*) All right, Roy. I'll see you back at the farm.

ALAN rises, PHILIPS also.

PHILIPS: Come with us – we'll pick your car up later.

ALAN: No; when I've seen Eric I'm driving over to Esher.

PHILIPS: (*Curious*) Esher?

ALAN: Carol's there … Someone's got to tell her about Harry Brent.

ALAN leaves the room. PHILIPS looks after him for a moment, then follows.

CUT TO: The living room of JACQUELINE DAWSON's flat.

ALAN is talking to CAROL who is standing by the window smoking a cigarette; she looks tense and drawn and has obviously been crying.

ALAN: I'm sorry I can't be more helpful, Carol.

CAROL: You've been very sweet, Alan, coming over here immediately like this … (*She moves to the table and stubs out her cigarette*) I do appreciate it (*Near to tears again*) But why did Eric go into the village when he had an appointment to see Harry? If he'd stayed at the house this would never have happened!

ALAN: I think it would, Carol. This man was determined to kill Harry, if not tonight, some other time.

ALAN moves closer to CAROL. There is a pause.

CAROL: How is Eric? I imagine he's very upset.

162

ALAN: Yes; it was a great shock, of course. He actually found Harry and the other man – Filey. I told him you were all right, by the way. I said I'd take you back there tonight.

CAROL: Thank you, Alan.

CAROL turns away from him, obviously distressed. ALAN hesitates, then puts his hand on her shoulder; he doesn't quite know what to say.

ALAN: Carol, believe me, I'm – terribly sorry about Harry, I … I just don't know what to say.

CAROL: There's nothing you can say, there's nothing anyone can … say … (*After a moment*) I – I – think I'd like a drink, Alan.

ALAN: Yes, of course.

ALAN turns to the drinks table and mixes CAROL a brandy and soda.

CAROL: Alan, don't you think someone ought to tell Miss Dawson and Mark Rainer about … tonight?

ALAN: I phoned the theatre and left a message. I've also spoken to one of our men, Superintendent Stenton. He works with the D.I. Five people.

CAROL nods. ALAN takes the drink to her.

ALAN: (*Hesitating*) Carol, this is hardly the time to talk to you about this, but …

CAROL looks at ALAN.

ALAN: This case will be taken out of my hands now – there's no doubt about that, it'll probably happen very quickly. (*He looks at Carol and hesitates*) I've got a hunch, Carol. It's only a hunch, but …

CAROL: Go on, Alan …

ALAN: I think I know who killed Harry. I think if they give me time, and you help me, Carol … I think I can nail the bastard …

CAROL: (*Puzzled*) But how can I help you, Alan?

163

There is a long pause. Alan is facing her; he looks serious, undecided.

ALAN: (*Quietly*) Sit down, Carol – and I'll tell you.

CAROL sits on the settee.

CUT TO: A corner table in the saloon bar of "The Bear Hotel", Market Weldon.

HAROLD TOLLY is sitting at the table reading a newspaper; there is a plate of sandwiches and a glass of beer in front of him. TOLLY is engrossed in the newspaper and doesn't immediately notice ALAN as, tankard in hand, he slips into the vacant chair at the table.

ALAN: Good morning, Mr Tolly.

TOLLY: (*Surprised*) Oh, hello, Inspector! That's damn funny, I've just been reading about you! I say – my God, what happened last night at Vyner's place?

ALAN: (*Indicating newspaper*) It's all there – I can't tell you any more than those boys.

TOLLY: The extraordinary thing is I saw Eric Vyner. I was with him until …

ALAN: Yes, I know. That's what I wanted to see you about. I understand you phoned him and asked him to meet you in Market Weldon?

TOLLY: No, he phoned me.

ALAN: He phoned you?

TOLLY: That's right. He's been trying to get some plants for me. He phoned me last night and said he'd got them. We started talking about the deal and then – well, to cut a long story short, we began haggling about the price, so I invited him down to my place to have a drink.

ALAN: What time was this?

TOLLY: About half past eight, I should imagine.

ALAN: You mean it was about half past eight when he arrived at your place?

TOLLY: No, that's when I phoned him. He got to the cottage about nine o'clock.

ALAN: And he stayed, how long?

TOLLY: Oh, I should think about an hour. Perhaps a little longer. (*Suddenly*) But surely to God you don't think Vyner had anything to do with this business?

ALAN: We don't know, Mr Tolly. But I'm very glad to hear that you don't think so. Right now you're a very important person so far as he's concerned.

TOLLY: Me? Important?

ALAN nods.

TOLLY: Why do you say that?

ALAN: According to the medical report, Harry Brent was murdered about nine-thirty, so if you're telling the truth …

TOLLY: Of course I'm telling the truth!

ALAN: … That let's Mr Vyner out.

TOLLY: Now I see what you're getting at! You mean – I'm his alibi?

ALAN picks up his tankard; is about to drink.

ALAN: That's right, Mr Tolly. You're his alibi. (*Pleasantly, almost an afterthought*) And he's yours, of course.

CUT TO: CAROL's Office at THOMAS FIELDING Ltd.
CAROL is sitting at the desk typing a letter, but her thoughts are elsewhere and after a moment she pulls the paper out of the machine and tosses it into the waste-paper basket. She rises from the desk and is reaching for a cigarette when the phone rings. CAROL looks at the phone, hesitates, then picks it up.

CAROL: … Miss Vyner's office …

ERIC's VOICE: Carol, this is Eric …

CAROL: (*Trying to control the tenseness in her voice*) Oh, hello, Eric …

CUT TO: The Office at Becklehurst Farm.

ERIC is standing by his desk. For the rest of this conversation we cut back and forth between ERIC and CAROL.

ERIC: Carol, I'm sorry to disturb you, but I thought I'd better let you know that Olive won't be back tonight. Her brother's taken a turn for the worse.

CAROL: Oh dear! I'm sorry. All right, Eric, thank you for letting me know. (*Suddenly*) Oh, Eric – I'd like your advice about something if you can spare a moment.

ERIC: Yes, of course.

CAROL: I was in Mr Fielding's office this morning going through some papers and I found a key. The key was to a deed-box. Mr Fielding showed me the box once, a long time ago, and … (*Hesitantly*) Perhaps I oughtn't to tell you this …

ERIC: (*Obviously interested*) What is it, Carol?

CAROL: I've found an envelope, it's marked "Urgent" and addressed to someone called Foster at the Ministry of Aviation.

ERIC: The Ministry of Aviation?

CAROL: Yes – what do you think I ought to do, Eric – post it to the Ministry or hand it over to the police?

ERIC: Hand the envelope over to the police, Carol. You can't go wrong if you do that. Give Alan a ring and tell him all about it.

CAROL: Yes, I think perhaps you're right, I'll do that. Thank you, Eric. See you later.

CAROL replaces the receiver and stands, deep in thought, staring down at the desk. After a moment she picks up a cigarette and lights it; as she puts down the lighter the door opens and ALAN enters. He wears outdoor clothes and is carrying a briefcase.

ALAN: I'm late, Carol! I'm awfully sorry, I've only just got back from London.

CAROL: (*Indicating the phone*) I'm afraid you've missed the performance. I've just this minute put the phone down.

ALAN: How did it go?

CAROL: I think it was all right. I hope so. I tried to sound convincing.

ALAN: I'm sure you were, Carol. (*Opens his briefcase*) Well – we shall soon know if my hunch was right or not.

ALAN takes an impressive looking envelope out of the case and puts it on the desk.

ALAN: Here's the envelope.

CAROL looks at the envelope, examining the seal.

CAROL: Well, this certainly looks important! (*She puts the envelope down*) How did you get on with the Superintendent?

ALAN: Not too bad, considering. He tore me off a strip and then said he'd hold his horses, for twenty-four hours at any rate. Miss Dawson was there, and another man from D.I.5, which was a help because they supported my request that …

The telephone starts to ring. CAROL looks at it.

CAROL: This is it. I told them I didn't want any other calls put through.

ALAN nods.

ALAN: (*Quietly*) Okay, Carol. Go ahead …

The phone continues ringing – then CAROL suddenly picks up the receiver. ALAN moves to the desk so that he can overhear what is being said.

CAROL: Miss Vyner's office …

Once again we cut back and forth between CAROL in her office and ERIC in his.

ERIC: Carol, this is Eric again, I'm sorry to disturb you …

CAROL: Oh, hello, Eric! Is anything the matter?

ERIC: No, no, it's just that I've had a phone call from Alan. He wants to see me and he's calling round here about half past one. I thought if you came home for lunch you could bring that envelope along with you and give it to him then.

CAROL: (*Looking at ALAN and nodding*) That's a very good idea, Eric …

ERIC: Don't worry about the bus, Carol – pick up a cab.

CAROL: Yes, all right. You'll have to excuse me, Eric. We're terribly busy at the moment.

ERIC: (*Pleasantly*) Yes, of course. Try not to be late, Carol.

CAROL: I'll do my best. Goodbye, Eric.

She slowly replaces the receiver and looks at ALAN.

ALAN: (*Quietly*) It worked.

CUT TO: Becklehurst Farm.

A taxi arrives at the farm and CAROL gets out of it carrying the sealed envelope. As she pays the driver, she notices ERIC watching her through the drawing room window. In the background near the bar, a group of men are loading bales of straw onto a huge lorry. DAVE WRIGHT, an athletic looking man in a polo neck sweater, is on the lorry, on top of the bales. He has a pitchfork in his hand and is issuing instructions to the men. An Austin-Healey 3000, and two or

168

three other cars are parked in the courtyard. CAROL looks across at the lorry as she walks towards the house.

CUT TO: The living room of Becklehurst Farm.
ERIC is standing near the door to his study awaiting the arrival of his sister. He is smoking a cigarette and   looks both worried and "on edge". CAROL enters: she has taken off her hat and coat but still carries the letter.

ERIC: Hello, Carol!
CAROL: Where's Alan – hasn't he arrived yet?
ERIC: No, and I'm afraid he's not coming. I had a phone call about ten minutes ago; he's had to go up to Town on important business.
CAROL: Oh. Oh, I see.
ERIC: He said he'd get in touch with me tomorrow morning. (*Hesitantly*) Is – that the letter you mentioned?
CAROL: Yes.
ERIC: I'd better put it in the safe, Carol.
CAROL: Yes, I think you'd better.
CAROL looks at ERIC as she offers him the envelope. He takes the letter and turns towards the study door.

CUT TO: ERIC VYNER's Study at Becklehurst Farm.
This is a small room, furnished as an Office. There is a leather armchair, filing cabinet, desk, etc. Two doors can be seen – one leading into an outside corridor, the other into the living room.
HAROLD TOLLY is standing close to the living room door, having just been listening to ERIC's conversation with CAROL. As the door opens, and ERIC enters the room, TOLLY flattens himself against the wall. ERIC closes the door and hands TOLLY the letter.

ERIC: Here it is …

TOLLY: (*Delighted*) Thank you, Mr Vyner. I congratulate
           you. I really couldn't have done better myself.

ERIC: (*Angrily*) You've got what you wanted, now get
           the hell out of here!

TOLLY: If you insist. But I'll be in touch.

TOLLY crosses to the door leading to the corridor.

CUT TO: The living room at Becklehurst Farm.

*CAROL is standing near the window looking out into the
courtyard. ERIC enters from the study and quickly crosses to
the phone. CAROL, without turning, still looks out of the
window.*

CAROL: Tolly's just come out of the house, he's going to
           the car …

ERIC: (*Dialling*) I hope to God I've got the right number
           …

CAROL: (*Turning*) Are you phoning Alan?

ERIC: Yes, he's waiting for the call – he's in the box
           opposite the drive … It's ringing now …
           (*Suddenly, on the phone*) Hello? Alan?

ALAN's VOICE: (*Over the phone*) Eric, what's happened?

ERIC: It's okay – he's just leaving!

*ERIC replaces the receiver and quickly joins CAROL at the
window.*

CUT TO: *Through the living room window TOLLY can be
seen driving the Austin-Healey away from the barn. He is
driving across the courtyard into the long drive leading up to
the main road. He looks pleased with himself as he leans
forward to switch on the car radio. Suddenly he hesitates, his
hand on the knob. Through the windscreen of the Austin-
Healy we can see a Police car entering the drive from the
main road. TOLLY looks tense and frightened. He brakes the*

170

car to a standstill, then quickly turns his head to see if there is anyone behind him. The drive is empty and TOLLY immediately starts to reverse his car back towards the house and courtyard. The Police car has now gained on the Austin-Healey and is within fifteen or twenty yards of TOLLY. TOLLY now realises that his best bet is to abandon the car: he brakes the Austin-Healy to a standstill, at the same time swinging the car across the drive so that it blocks the pursuing Police car. TOLLY quickly takes a gun from the glove compartment and then opens the car door and jumps down onto the drive. The Police car has stopped and one of the uniformed men – SMITHSON – is already on the drive, ready to give chase after TOLLY. TOLLY is running down the drive towards the courtyard. He turns and, seeing the four occupants of the Police car – ALAN, PHILIPS, SMITHSON and LUNT – in hot pursuit, fires the gun. ALAN is making his way past the Austin-Healey when the bullet from TOLLY's gun shatters the windscreen of the stationary car. ALAN quickly drops down, sheltering behind the car. TOLLY has now reached the entrance to the courtyard and he turns and fires the fun again in the direction of the Police car and his pursuers. LUNT has been hit in the arm by the second bullet and he falls back against the wire fence bordering the drive. PHILIPS rushes towards him. In the background, two Police cars can be seen entering the drive from the main road. TOLLY is in the courtyard, hesitating – taking stock of his surroundings – wondering which way to run. The men loading the lorry have stopped work and are staring at TOLLY in amazement. As TOLLY makes a decision and races towards the barn, ALAN arrives in the courtyard, followed by PHILIPS and SMITHSON. TOLLY turns and raises the gun; as he does so one of the farm workers rushes at him in an attempt to bring him to the ground. TOLLY quickly hits the man on the side of the head with the gun – as the man falls the

171

other farm workers close in on TOLLY who faces them, gun in hand. He looks angry and desperate. ALAN and PHILIPS have stopped dead in their tracks. They are watching TOLLY, anxiously wondering whether he is going to use the gun again. TOLLY backs towards the lorry – faced by the group of angry farm workers. The man on the ground slowly rises, rubbing the back of his head and glaring across at TOLLY as he does so. On the lorry, DAVE WRIGHT, standing on the bales of straw, has been overlooked by TOLLY. As TOLLY falls back towards the lorry, DAVE glances across at ALAN – finally catching his eye. ALAN gives a hardly perceptible nod. DAVE crouches, ready to spring from the lorry onto TOLLY below. The Austin-Healey suddenly appears, being reversed out of the drive by a policeman. Police cars follow, sweeping into the courtyard. Through the living room window – ERIC and CAROL are anxiously watching the turn of events. They see the arrival of the Police cars and, in the distance, DAVE on the lorry preparing to jump. The arrival of Police reinforcements takes TOLLY by surprise. He decides to take the final gamble and make a dash for the barn – at the precise moment DAVE jumps from the lorry ... As DAVE falls on TOLLY, bringing him to the ground, ALAN rushes forward, closely followed by PHILIPS and the farm workers.

CUT TO: ALAN MILTON's Office At C.I.D. Headquarters.
ALAN is sitting at his desk talking to ROY PHILIPS.

ALAN: … Tolly killed his wife because she was getting out of hand and talking too much. Also, she'd far too many boyfriends. Tolly didn't mind this, but it was a dangerous situation once he became mixed up with the really big stuff like the Fielding affair.

PHILIPS: Yes, I can see that. But I still don't understand what happened the night Harry Brent was killed.

ALAN: Eric was friendly with Phyllis Tolly. Her husband knew this and started to blackmail him. On Thursday night Tolly phoned Eric and asked him to go down to his cottage. Eric went, but Tolly, of course, wasn't there – he was at the farm waiting for Harry. (*He rises from his desk*) Eric was frightened, so frightened that he decided to tell me about his relationship with Mrs Tolly. I took a gamble and with Eric's help – and Carol's – laid a trap. Tolly was invited to the farm and deliberately allowed to "overhear" a phone conversation with Carol. You know what happened. He told Eric to ring her back and get the letter.

PHILIPS: Yes, but when did you first suspect Tolly – when did you first realise he was X?

ALAN: I began to get suspicious when he said he'd changed his mind, and now wanted to tell me the truth. I had a feeling that wasn't his real reason for coming to see me – or the photograph he produced. I felt convinced they were both just excuses, in fact. Later on, of course, when Jason escaped …

PHILIPS: You realised you were right. It was Tolly that planted the gun.

ALAN: Yes, and that was the reason – the only reason – why he came here. (*Moving towards PHILIPS*) Tolly was worried about Kevin Jason, even perhaps a little scared of him.

The door opens and TOMLINS enters.

ALAN: You knew darn well there was always the chance that the Irishman might talk, and if that happened …

TOMLINS: Excuse me, sir. You asked me to let you know when Miss Vyner was leaving.

ALAN: Oh, yes! Has the Superintendent finished with her?

TOMLINS: Yes, sir. She's signed the statement – everything's in order and she's just about to leave.

ALAN: (*Briskly*) Thank you, Tomlins. (*To PHILIPS*) I'll be back in five minutes.

ALAN goes out of the office. TOMLINS looks at PHILIPS and grins.

CUT TO: Outside C.I.D. Headquarters.

CAROL has just left the building, and is thoughtfully walking towards the path when ALAN suddenly appears in the doorway.

ALAN: Carol!

CAROL: (*Turning*) Oh, hello, Alan …

ALAN joins her.

CAROL: I didn't want to disturb you, I thought perhaps you were busy.

ALAN looks at her. She looks away.

CAROL: Was the statement all right?

ALAN: Yes, of course. I'm sorry I had to drag you down here, but the Superintendent insisted. Are you going back to the office?

CAROL: Yes.

ALAN: I'll run you there.

CAROL: I'd just as soon walk.

ALAN: All right then, I'll walk with you.

CAROL: No, Alan, please … I'd rather be alone.

ALAN: (*After a moment*) … If that's want you want, Carol. (*Looking at CAROL*) I'll phone you one day next week.

CAROL: Yes, do that – please do that, Alan.

CAROL looks at him, then with an affectionate nod turns away. ALAN stands watching her as she walks down the path.

THE END

But that's not quite the end of the Harry Brent story. When German tv station WDR decided to make their own version of the serial for several reasons they wanted changes making to Francis Durbridge's original script.

We print here the reply Francis Durbridge sent to Dr Gunther Rohrbach at WDR:

Dear Dr Rohrbach,

Thank you very much for your kind letter dated 28th September and my apologies for not having replied sooner. I have been extremely busy and I have also been away for several days.

I have now given careful thought to your request concerning the death of Harry Brent in my serial. Naturally, I feel that my present ending is the correct one for the story, otherwise of course I would never have written the serial this way in the first instance. Nevertheless, since you apparently feel very strongly that your viewers should be spared the death of this character then I will of course help you out in this matter and make the suggested alteration for you. I hope to let Mrs De Barde have the revised ending within the next three or four weeks. Earlier, if possible.

I think, in view of this change to the end of the German presentation of the story, it might be a good idea for you to change the title of the serial and also the names of the main characters. The reason I suggest this is because the play has been presented, with considerable success, in several other countries under the present title "A Man Called Harry Brent" and with of course my original end. However, this is purely a matter for you to decide. I will send you a list of new character names with the new material just in case this idea should appeal to you.

177

With kindest regards and, as always, my very best wishes.

Sincerely yours,

WDR did not change the name of the serial but did change the names of some of the characters as follows:

BBC-Version	WDR-Version
HARRY BRENT	HARRY BRENT
ALAN MILTON	JAMES WALLACE
DET. SGT. ROY PHILIPS	SERGEANT ROY PHILIPS
CAROL VYNER	JANE CONWAY
ERIC VYNER	GEORGE CONWAY
HAROLD TOLLY	WILLIAM BROTHER
MRS TOLLY	PHYLLIS BROTHER
THOMAS FIELDING	SAM FIELDING

The German Ending

This script commences after HARRY BRENT has been stabbed in the barn (see page 160).

BRENT is stabbed in the barn. He falls to the ground.

CUT TO: A STREET AT NIGHT.
An ambulance drives through the dark night.

CUT TO: INSIDE THE AMBULANCE.
We see FILEY lying on top of a stretcher, HARRY BRENT is on a lower stretcher.
A NURSE measures HARRY's pulse and looks at her watch. Then she turns to the driver.

NURSE: If you hurry, there's a chance we can save him.

CUT TO: THE PUB.
INSPECTOR WALLACE sits at a table and eats. GLADYS serves him an ice cream sundae.

GLADYS: There we are.

WALLACE: (*Amazed*) Oh, thank you, Gladys.

WALLACE enjoys drinking his beer and picks up the spoon to eat the sundae.
SERGEANT PHILIPS enters the restaurant and looks around. He goes to the bar, then he sees INSPECTOR WALLACE. He walks up to the table, takes off his hat and sits down. WALLACE continues to eat the sundae with relish.

PHILIPS: I've been looking for you everywhere!

WALLACE doesn't say a word but continues to eat the ice cream.

PHILIPS: You weren't in your flat either.

WALLACE: I do have to eat sometimes. (*He takes another spoonful of ice cream. He speaks with a full mouth:*) What's happened?

PHILIPS: (*Looking around to ensure no one else is listening*) Someone tried to kill Harry Brent.

WALLACE: (*Surprised*) What?

181

PHILIPS: George Conway found him, with a knife in his chest, in the barn. Next to him lay a man named Filey. He's dead. A bullet in his stomach.

WALLACE: And Brent?

PHILIPS: He's been taken to the hospital in Kingston. Had two emergency operations. He's still on the danger list. Looks like Brent was attacked by this Filey character and then Filey got shot. And then... (*Hesitates*)

WALLACE: Well?

PHILIPS: But this is just a theory of mine...

WALLACE: Go on ...!

PHILIPS: Then a third party appeared on the scene!

WALLACE: (*Nods*) Yes, yes, that's certainly possible!

PHILIPS: Conway says he was expecting Harry Brent, but then William Brother called him and he had to go to Guildford. When he came back, Brent's car was in the yard, but he couldn't get in the house because all the doors were locked, so he searched the yard and finally found him in the barn. Conway is pretty much done.

WALLACE stands up.

WALLACE: O.K., let's go! Gladys! My bill, please!

PHILIPS also gets up and both leave.

CUT TO: JACQUELINE DAWSON'S LIVING ROOM.

JANE CONWAY sits desperately on the sofa, holding her head in her hand.

WALLACE: I was just on the phone to the hospital before I left.

JANE looks up at WALLACE expectantly.

JANE: And?

182

WALLACE: Well... They never tell you anything exactly,
             but... he's alive, Jane! And he's not one to
             give up easily!

JANE says nothing. She takes a cigarette out of the case.

JANE: What does George say?

WALLACE: He's very confused. I've told him that you're
             all right and promised to take you back
             tonight!

*JANE puts the cigarette in her mouth without lighting it, gets
up and walks around.*

WALLACE: Jane, this may seem trivial to you now, but...

JANE: What about Mrs. Dawson?

WALLACE: What? Mrs. Dawson... Oh yes... Yes, when do
             you expect her back?

JANE: After tonight's performance. She said she'd
             leave straight after the curtain call.

WALLACE: We can call her – let her know what has
             happened. Jane... (*He turns off the light of the
             floor lamp*) ... This case will no doubt be
             taken out of my hands, probably immediately.
             I have the feeling...

JANE: What?

WALLACE: I think I know who wanted to kill Brent!

JANE: Who?

WALLACE: If they give me the time and you help me...

JANE: But how am I supposed to help you?

WALLACE: Listen...

CUT TO: IN THE INN.

*INSPECTOR WALLACE comes in and goes to the bar where
GLADYS is serving.*

WALLACE: Gladys, give me a beer!

*GLADYS pours him a beer. WALLACE looks around and sees
WILLIAM BROTHER sitting in a corner, reading a*

newspaper and eating something. WALLACE crosses to him
and sits down.

WALLACE: Good day, Mr. Brother!

BROTHER: (*Indifferently*) Good day, Inspector! (*Pointing to the newspaper*) I'm reading about you, right now! About what happened at Becklehurst last night. (*He puts the newspaper down*) What happened?

WALLACE: It's all there in the paper, that's all I can tell you.

BROTHER: Strange. I was with George Conway around that time yesterday.

WALLACE: Yes, I know. And I wanted to talk to you about that.

BROTHER nods and takes a sip of his beer.

WALLACE: If I'm properly informed, you called him and asked him to come to see you.

BROTHER: No, he called me.

WALLACE: Oh, he called you?

BROTHER: Yes, we wanted to make a supply contract with each other. I need his vegetables and he needs money... and then he called last night and said, we had to talk again about the price and the contract. We didn't agree right away and I said: "We have to negotiate this at home with a whisky."

WALLACE: Aha. What time was that?

BROTHER: Around half past nine, I should say.

WALLACE: So around half past nine he came to see you.

BROTHER: No, we talked on the phone. He came to see me about nine.

WALLACE: How long did he stay?

BROTHER: (*Eating his sandwich as he speaks*) An hour
maybe, maybe a bit longer... Say you don't
think Conway has anything to do with this?

WALLACE: We don't know, Mr. Brother, but right now
you're extremely important to him.

BROTHER: Me? Why?

WALLACE: The autopsy shows that Filey was murdered
around half past ten. Around the same time,
Brent probably got stabbed. So if you're telling
the truth...

BROTHER: (*Offended*) Of course I'm telling the truth!

WALLACE: ... George Conway is relieved!

BROTHER: Oh? So I'm his alibi, so to speak?

WALLACE: (Laughs) Yes, that's right, Mr. Brother. (*He
takes a sip of beer*) And he's yours, of course!

BROTHER looks puzzled and takes a sip of beer.

CUT TO: FIELDING'S OFFICE. JANE's OFFICE /
GEORGE CONWAY'S LIVING ROOM.
*JANE CONWAY is sitting behind her desk. The phone rings.
The following telephone conversation cuts between the two
places.*

JANE: Conway?

CONWAY: (*Visibly nervous*) Jane, I just wanted to tell
you, Olive isn't coming back tonight.

*In the background at CONWAY's we can see a shadow and
hear the footsteps of someone who is impatiently walking up
and down. GEORGE CONWAY is obviously very nervous.*

JANE: Oh dear, hopefully she won't stay out too
long. But it's a good thing you called,
George, I wanted to ask you something
anyway. I looked through a few files and
found a key to a deed box belonging to Sam

185

	Fielding. And in the box there's... but maybe I shouldn't do anything at all about it.
CONWAY:	Jane, tell me! What is it? What's in the box?
JANE:	There's a letter in there, a thick envelope, it says "urgent" and it's addressed to a Mr. Foster in the Ministry of Aviation...
CONWAY:	(*Surprised*) The Ministry of Aviation?
JANE:	Yes! What do you think I should do with it? Send it or hand over to the police?
CONWAY:	Hand it over to the police, that will be best! Call James and let him know!
JANE:	Yes, well, if that's what you think I should do. Thank you. See you later, George.

CONWAY hangs up. He looks worried.

JANE sits thoughtfully behind the desk. There is a knock on the door and INSPECTOR WALLACE comes in.

WALLACE:	Sorry, I've just come back from London!
JANE:	You missed my performance. I just made the phone call.
WALLACE:	(*Curious*) How did it go?
JANE:	Quite well, I think. I hope I sounded convincing.

WALLACE sits down on the chair in front of JANE's desk.

JANE:	In any case, I tried very hard!
WALLACE:	(*Opening his briefcase*) You've done a brilliant job! Well... we will soon know if I was right. (*He takes a large envelope out of his briefcase*) Here!
JANE:	That looks like something important!
WALLACE:	I think so too.
JANE:	How did your talk with the Commissioner go?
WALLACE:	Oh, not too bad. At first he wasn't too friendly. He grilled me pretty thoroughly, but

then he gave me another day to resolve everything. Jacqueline Dawson was also there and then someone from Harry's department arrived. That was very convenient for me because they both supported me and my proposal.

The phone rings. Both look up with a start.

JANE: This is it. I told the switchboard they shouldn't put through any other calls.

INSPECTOR WALLACE raises his crossed fingers.

WALLACE: Go on! Answer it!

JANE looks at him resolutely and lifts the telephone receiver.
WALLACE gets up and listens to the conversation.

JANE: Sam Fielding's office, Jane Conway speaking.

CONWAY: Jane? It's me again... Sorry... James just called me. He wants to speak to me. He's coming here at half past two.

While CONWAY is on the phone, the other person in the room continues to go up and down in the background, but we only hear their footsteps and do not see them. CONWAY seems to fix his stare on the unknown person during the telephone conversation.

CONWAY: You said you were coming home for lunch. Bring the envelope with you and give it to James then.

WALLACE nods to JANE.

JANE: Yes, good idea, George, I'll do that.

CONWAY: Don't wait long for the bus. Take a taxi.

JANE: Yes, all right. But I have to go now. I'm really up to my eyes in it here.

CONWAY: (*Emphatically*) Get here as soon as you can!

JANE: I'll do my best. See you, George!

JANE hangs up.

187

WALLACE: There we go!

JANE takes the envelope and gets up and leaves.
INSPECTOR WALLACE follows her.

CUIT TO: COURTYARD OF GEORGE CONWAY'S ESTATE.
A taxi pulls up, JANE gets out, holding the envelope in her hand. GEORGE CONWAY watches her through the window. JANE pays the taxi driver and then goes towards the house, seeing a strange car standing in front of the house as she goes.

CUT TO: GEORGE CONWAY'S HOUSE. THE HALL.
CONWAY opens the door. JANE enters.

CONWAY: Here you are, Jane!
JANE: Isn't James here yet?
CONWAY: No. No. He isn't coming, I'm afraid. He called a quarter of an hour ago to say that he needed to go urgently to London...
JANE: Oh no...
CONWAY: He said he'd get back to you tomorrow.
JANE: O.K.

JANE is nervous. She hands over the envelope to CONWAY. CONWAY is also visibly nervous.

CONWAY: That's the letter?
JANE: Yes.
CONWAY: I'd better put it in the safe right away.
JANE: Yes! That's probably best.

CONWAY nods and nervously opens the door to the living room.

CONWAY: Are you coming in here first?
JANE: (*Nervously but trying not to show it*) Yes.

JANE quickly goes into the room. CONWAY looks at the envelope and closes the door behind Jane, stopping in the hallway. Then he goes to the stairs and looks up to the first-floor landing. He gives someone a sign that they should come. Someone comes down the stairs. CONWAY gives them the envelope.

CONWAY: Here you are – now don't bother me again

Now we can see that the other person is WILLIAM BROTHER. He grabs the envelope and is in a hurry.

BROTHER: That's what I want! And if you think that's an
            end to it as far as you're concerned you can
            think again!

CUT TO: IN GEORGE CONWAY'S LIVING ROOM.

JANE CONWAY stands at the window and looks out as GEORGE CONWAY enters the room. JANE turns to face CONWAY.

JANE: James is standing at the gates with his people.

CONWAY walks to the window, looks out in fear and pushes JANE aside.

CONWAY: Get away from the window!

CUT TO: COURTYARD OF GEORGE CONWAY'S ESTATE.

WILLIAM BROTHER hurriedly leaves the house and sprints to his car. He looks around quickly and then gets in. He places the envelope on the passenger seat. He turns the car, drives to the courtyard exit. But INSPECTOR WALLACE and SERGEANT PHILIPS face him. WALLACE signals with his hand that BROTHER should stop. But BROTHER presses on the accelerator so that WALLACE and PHILIPS have to jump to the side. BROTHER races to the driveway, but a police car blocks his way. BROTHER breaks and reverses the car so that he can turn it round. He drives across the yard and gets a revolver out of the glove compartment. But the other courtyard exit is also blocked by a police car. BROTHER jumps out of the car with the revolver.

WALLACE: (*Shouting*) Stop, Mr. Brother!

BROTHER doesn't react. Police officers are now approaching him from all sides. WALLACE and PHILIPS approach him. BROTHER shoots. WALLACE shoots back. Both miss their target. BROTHER shoots again and hits a farm employee who wants to stop him.

WALLACE: (*Out of shot*) Stop, Brother! You're only making things worse for yourself!

BROTHER takes refuge in a barn that is full of agricultural machinery and runs up a flight of stairs. A POLICEMAN follows him. BROTHER shoots him and the POLICEMAN falls down. Then BROTHER continues his escape. He tries to escape through a roof hatch, but it is too dangerous for him.

JANE CONWAY runs out of the house, followed by GEORGE CONWAY.

CONWAY: Stay inside, it's too dangerous!

BROTHER runs over the roof of the building, the envelope still in his hands. He forces two policemen, with the gun in his hand, to retreat. But police officers are also approaching him from the other side. The noose tightens. PHILIPS opens a hatch in the roof and tries to shoot at BROTHER, but BROTHER realises it and shoots back. PHILIPS disappears into the hatch. BROTHER sprints out of the window, underneath which is a trailer loaded with hay. He lands softly on the hay. A CIVILIAN OFFICER jumps after him and pulls him to the ground.

WALLACE: Give it up, Brother, you don't stand a chance!

More police officers are jumping in and holding BROTHER. WALLACE is able to snatch the gun from him from below. BROTHER fights back fiercely.

CUT TO: IN THE HOSPITAL. HARRY BRENT'S ROOM.
HARRY BRENT lies in bed, WALLACE sits in front of it.

BRENT: So it was Brother! (*To WALLACE*) But why does a man like him get involved in a thing like that? He had a good living.

WALLACE: Not always. Brother was on the verge of bankruptcy a few years ago and that's why he got involved so easily and became an easy victim and a sort of fall guy with the espionage ring.

BRENT: Then he also has his wife on his conscience?

WALLACE: Yes. After Fielding was murdered, she refused to go on. And when she came to me, her fate was sealed.

BRENT: And who was the second man the night before yesterday in Becklehurst?

WALLACE: It was Brother himself. He wanted to make sure that Brent was dealt with that time after Filey had messed up before. He asked George to his place and just made him wait half an hour.

BRENT: But ... How did George get involved in all this?

WALLACE: Brother blackmailed him. George was having an affair with Phyllis Brother. And Brother threatened to make a scandal. And what that would have meant for George's sick wife, you can imagine... But when he found you unconscious in his yard, he came to me. Luckily still in time to help you.

BRENT: When did you actually start to suspect Brother?

WALLACE: Well... (*Taking off his hat and putting it on BRENT's bed*) Actually quite early on. But due to his clever trick with the fountain pen and the two hundred pounds alleged advance from Kevin Jason, I wasn't sure for a while. It wasn't until we found Jason's body that everything suddenly became clear to me. Jason had apparently been eliminated because he shouldn't be allowed to testify under any circumstances. That's why Brother came to me that day. He just needed an official reason to be in the police station and help Jason escape. And of course, knowing that Jason would disappear forever, he could incriminate him as much as he wanted. Because he knew he was going to be eliminated.

BRENT: Yes, but if something had gone wrong with the escape...

WALLACE: Well. That was his risk. However, it was...

The door opens and a SISTER comes in. She has a tray with a glass of water and tablets with her. WALLACE stands up.

SISTER: Excuse me, Inspector, but there's another visitor outside waiting to come in.

She goes to Brent and gives him the tablets.

SISTER: (*To HARRY*) But first you have to take these!

WALLACE: I'd better be going... See you later... And get well soon, (*He hesitates and laughs*)... Harry!

BRENT: Thank you very much... (*He also hesitates, then friendly*) ... James!

BRENT swallows the tablets.

OUTSIDE OF THE HOSPITAL ROOM.

JANE sits on a bench and eats chocolates from a bag. WALLACE comes out of the room. JANE looks up in surprise.

JANE: Oh, James, what are you doing here?

192

WALLACE:	He wanted to talk to me – know what was going on.
JANE:	(*In a good mood*) How's he doing?
WALLACE:	He's o.k. The sister says he's made great progress in the last 24 hours.

The SISTER comes out of the room.

SISTER:	You can go in now, Miss Conway!

JANE gets up.

JANE:	Thank you, sister.

JANE wants to open the door, but WALLACE also gets up and stops her.

WALLACE:	I'll wait for you and then take you home.
JANE:	Thank you, James, but I want to... I still want to go to the office.
WALLACE:	Well, then I'll take you to the office.
JANE:	Oh, that's not necessary. I can take the train.
WALLACE:	Well, then I'll take you to the train station.
JANE:	(*Smiles*) No, no, I... um... I think... I think I'd prefer to walk. Don't be annoyed with me...
WALLACE:	(Persistently) Well, then we'll go on foot!
JANE:	(*Laughs*) Please, James... I'd prefer to go alone!
WALLACE:	(*Understandingly*) Oh, o.k. ... So, can I call you!
JANE:	Yes. Please, James!

JANE goes into the room. WALLACE stops briefly and thinks, then leaves and stops again. He turns around and looks thoughtful.

IN THE HOSPITAL ROOM.

BRENT lies in bed, JANE sits on the bed. They kiss.

BRENT:	Have you seen James yet?
JANE:	(*Indifferently*) Yes.

JANE gets up and goes to the mirror. She straightens her hair.

BRENT: He offered to take you home, didn't he?

JANE doesn't give an answer, takes the comb and straightens her hairstyle.

JANE: How are you?

BRENT: Thank you, much better. I'm making rapid progress.

JANE turns around, something is obviously on her mind.

JANE: There's something else I wanted to know.

BRENT: Yes. I know. The answer is: Yes!

JANE: (*Doesn't understand, questioning*) Yes? What do you mean?

BRENT: (*Laughs*) I got to know you because you were busy with Fielding. He recommended my travel agency to you because I asked him to. (*Laughs*) I had no idea I was going to fall in love with you.

JANE in close-up. She smiles and looks in love.

IN THE HOSPITAL CORRIDOR.

INSPECTOR WALLACE sits on the bench where JANE sat earlier. He sits there and eats the chocolates that JANE left there. The SISTER comes through a door and walks past him.

SISTER: (*In passing*) Weren't those meant for the patient, Inspector! There's nothing wrong with you, is there?

WALLACE: No? I wouldn't be so sure, sister.

He puts another praline in his mouth.

THE END

Printed in Great Britain
by Amazon